LITTLE DOOMSDAYS

NIC LOW

and

PHIL DADSON

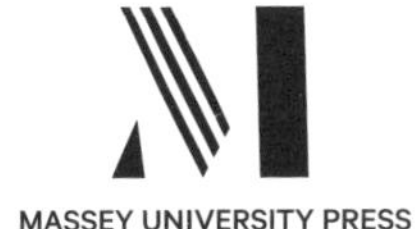

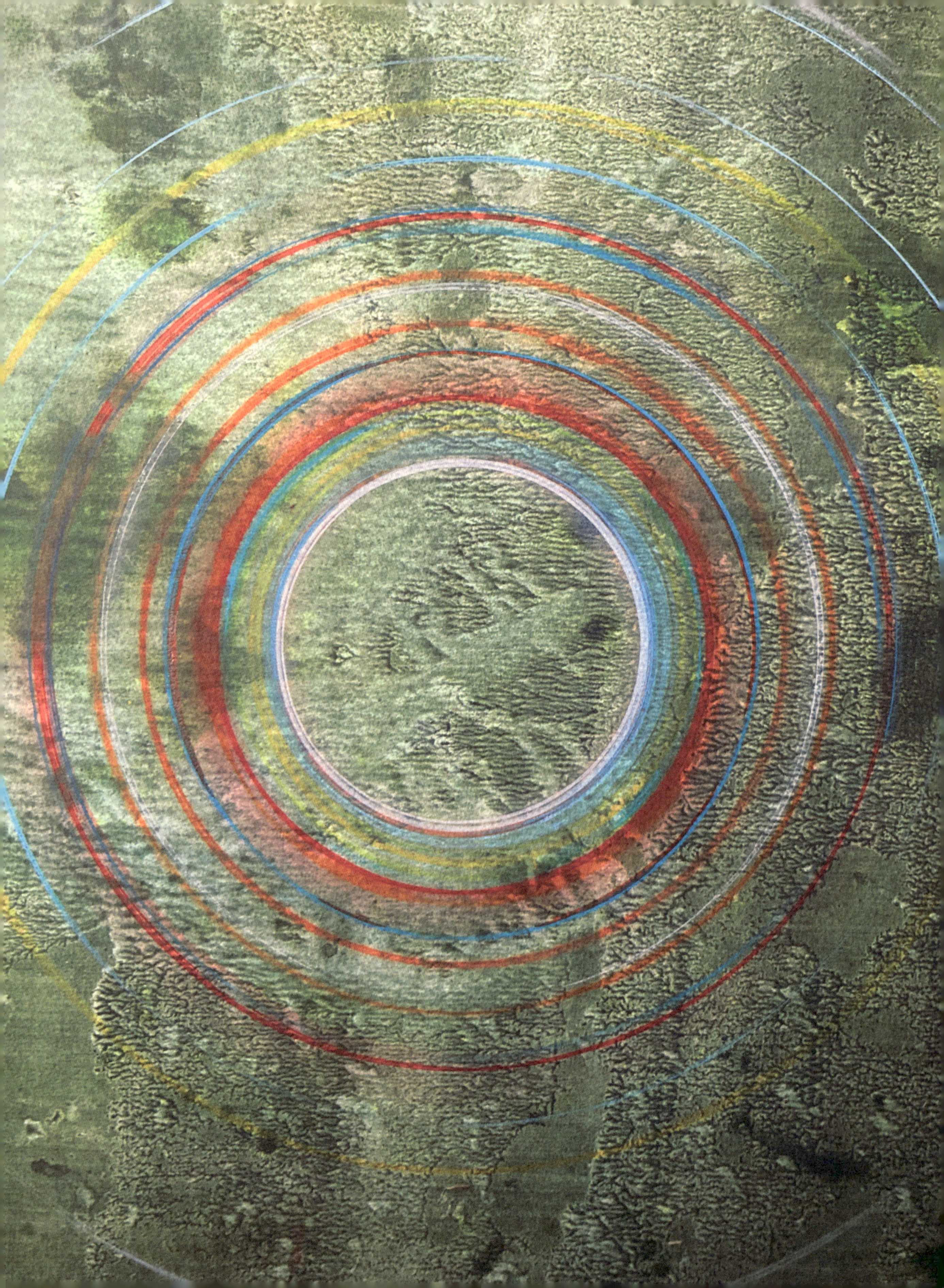

E kore au e ngaro, he kākano ahau i ruia mai i Rangiātea.
I can never be lost; I am a seed sown from Rangiātea.

It's said — in the quiet between buses, down the back of the pub, in the hushed elevator rising to the penthouse — that in the late twentieth century an unstable grouping of scholars, writers and fanatics from several Ngāi Tahu hapū in Murihiku created what has come to be known as the Ark of Arks.

It's said that this project, ill-conceived and poorly executed as it was, aimed to catalogue all known arks from the last five millennia.

It was a failed attempt to capture previous civilisations' failed attempts to preserve whatever was valuable to them: waka huia, time capsules, caches, burial ships, seed banks, languages, objects and data.

The Ark of Arks was, in itself, useless. But not without merit.

It is said to contain a complete inventory of the waka *Horouta* on its colonising voyage from Hawaiki to Aotearoa, down to the grains of sand lodged in the hems of the sails, and the whakapapa of those grains of sand.

It is said to contain a complete inventory of the biblical ark.

It is said to contain the hopes of those who have moved past denial and mitigation to open fear.

It is said that the Ark of Arks was compiled immediately before the last flood.

The people of the whare wānaka, the house of sacred learning, gathered their knowledge onto a dozen hard drives and placed them inside a lead-lined stainless-steel waka huia.

It's said they built the great wharenui at Ōraka, where the spirit of Tūterakiwhānoa resides.

If that wharenui still stands above the waves, go to Ōraka and walk around the walls, the likes of which have not been seen before, or since.

Examine the carved pou that hold up the spine of that house; be watched by the ancestors' eyes that flash like --------.

Inside, lay your hands on the pou tokomanawa. Admire the carving. Inhale the tōtara resin fresh from the chisel's blade — though the wood is older than the dead at Pūharakeke-tapu.

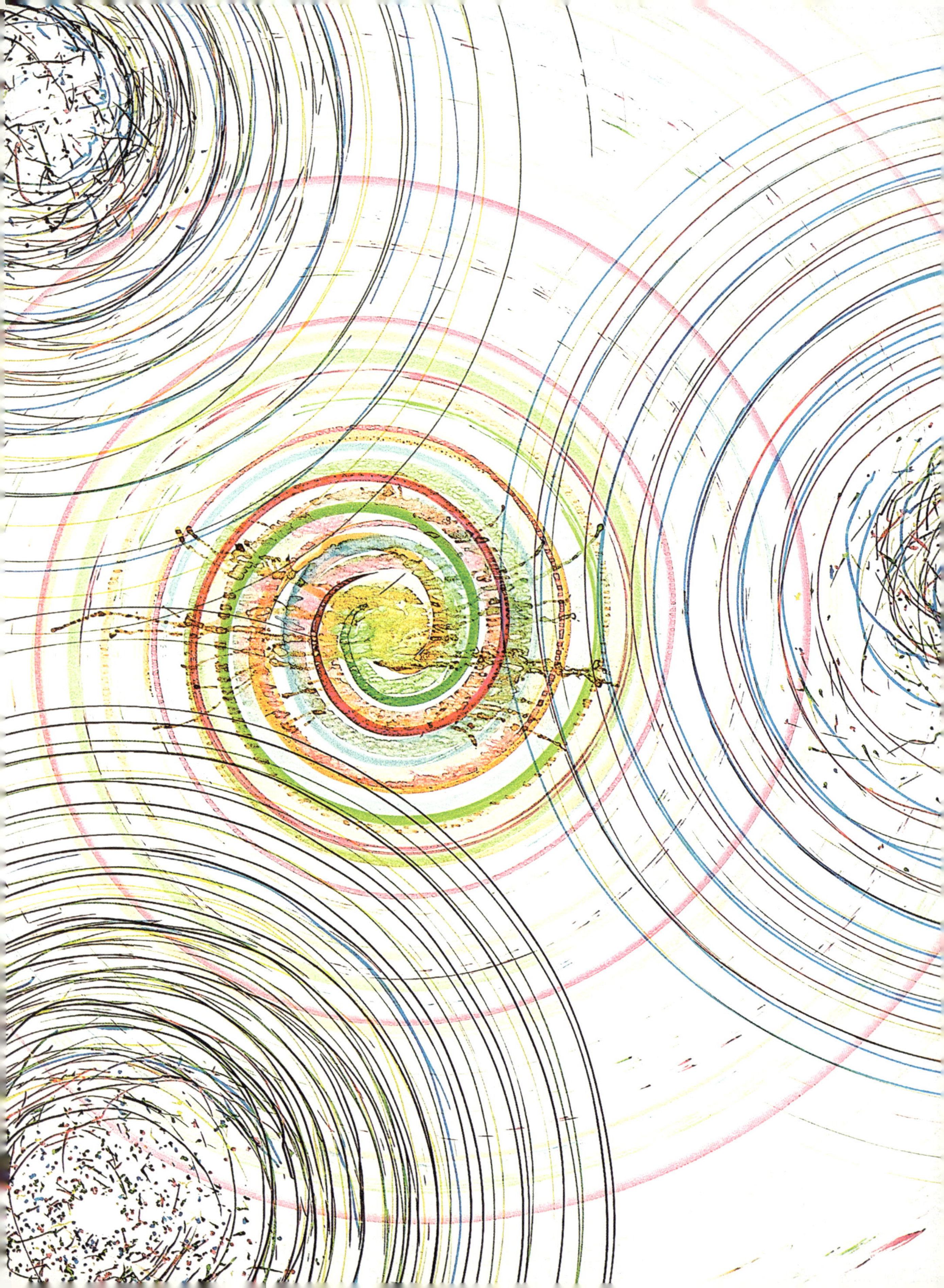

At the base of the pou, search until you find where the stainless-steel waka huia is lodged. Open the tungsten lock and decipher the ingenious mechanism by which it unfolds.

Take out the screens, power them up and begin to read.

The first line of the Ark of Arks reads: **E kore au e ngaro, he kākano ahau i ruia mai i Rangiātea.**

And the second: **I can never be lost; I am a seed sown from Rangiātea.**

The third: **It's said — in the quiet between buses, down the back of the pub, in the hushed elevator rising to the penthouse — that in the late twentieth century an unstable grouping of scholars, writers and fanatics from several Ngāi Tahu hapū in Murihiku created what has come to be known as the Ark of Arks.**

You will be told to visit the great wharenui at Ōraka and to find the stainless-steel waka huia. You are to take out the screens and power them up. As you have just done.

You have found the Ark of Arks. You are reading it now.

We have found you, at last.

◎

Entry 34CH4D: Fragments of clay tablet, 2100 BCE

It is said that in the 1860s, George Smith earned his keep in London as an engraver of bank notes.

It is said that his other more notable skills in reading ancient languages were self-taught.

It is said he spent his days in that great repository of stolen property, the British Museum, hunched over fragments of clay tablets unearthed from ancient Nineveh, nowadays Mosul in Iraq.

It is said that in 1866 George Smith began translating a sequence of fragments that revealed the history of a man named Uta-napishti.

The gods warned Uta-napishti of a coming flood.

Uta-napishti built a cube-shaped ark, one acre by one acre by one acre. He gathered domestic and wild animals, and skilled craftspeople and his whānau, and set sail the day before water covered the Earth.

The fragments said this flood drowned all living things except Uta-napishti and his charges.

It's said that when George Smith translated these words, and their meaning sank in, he threw back his chair and ran through the echoing halls of the great museum, tearing off his clothes.

Those fine cuneiform letters, so like birdprints in wet sand, seemed to prove the truth of Genesis. The biblical flood was real.

Except that Uta-napishti wasn't Noah. It was the other way round.

Smith had found the Epic of Gilgamesh: the earliest work of written literature, the source of the story of Noah's flood.

Clay was the ark that preserved the ark.

◎

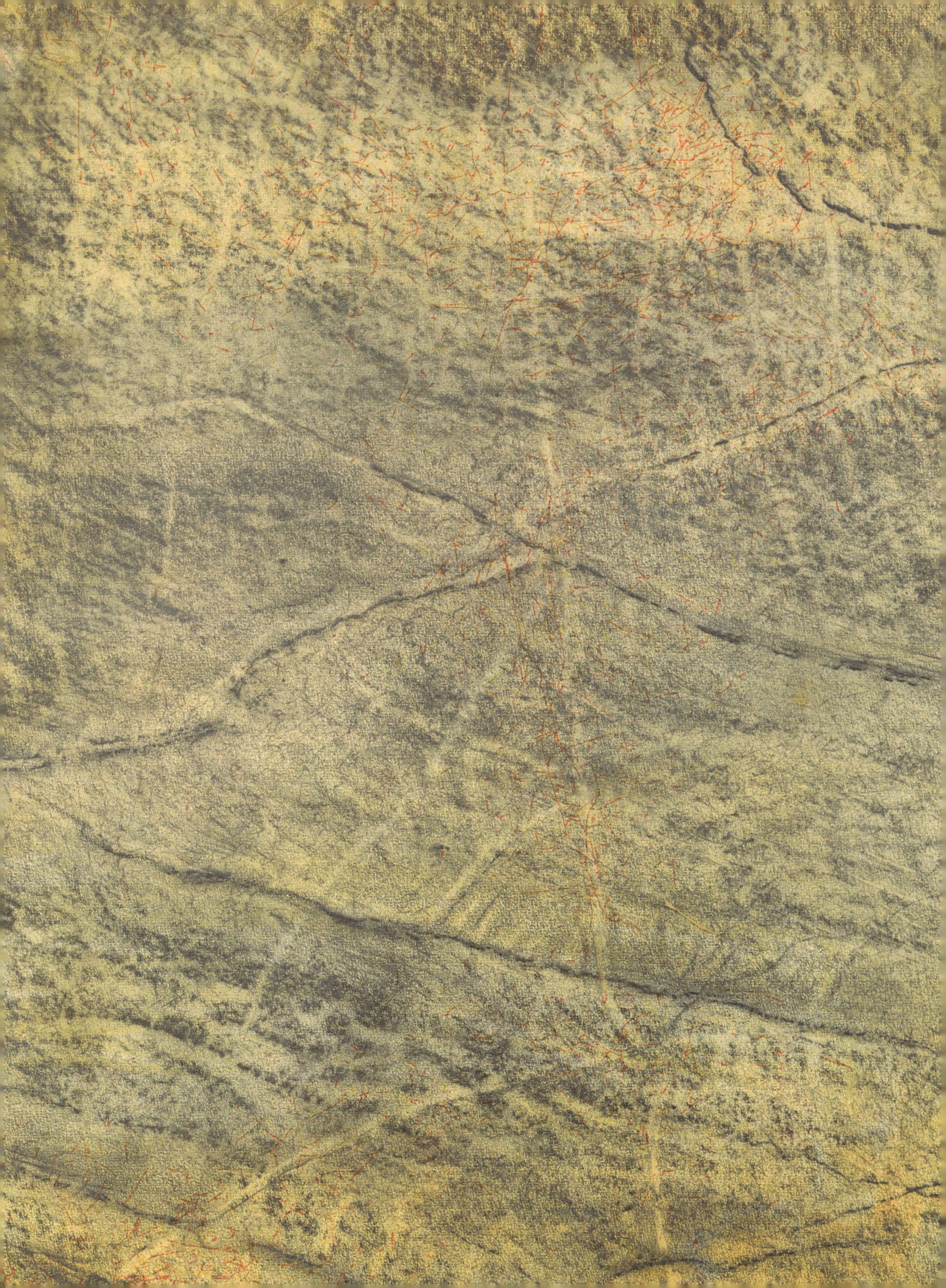

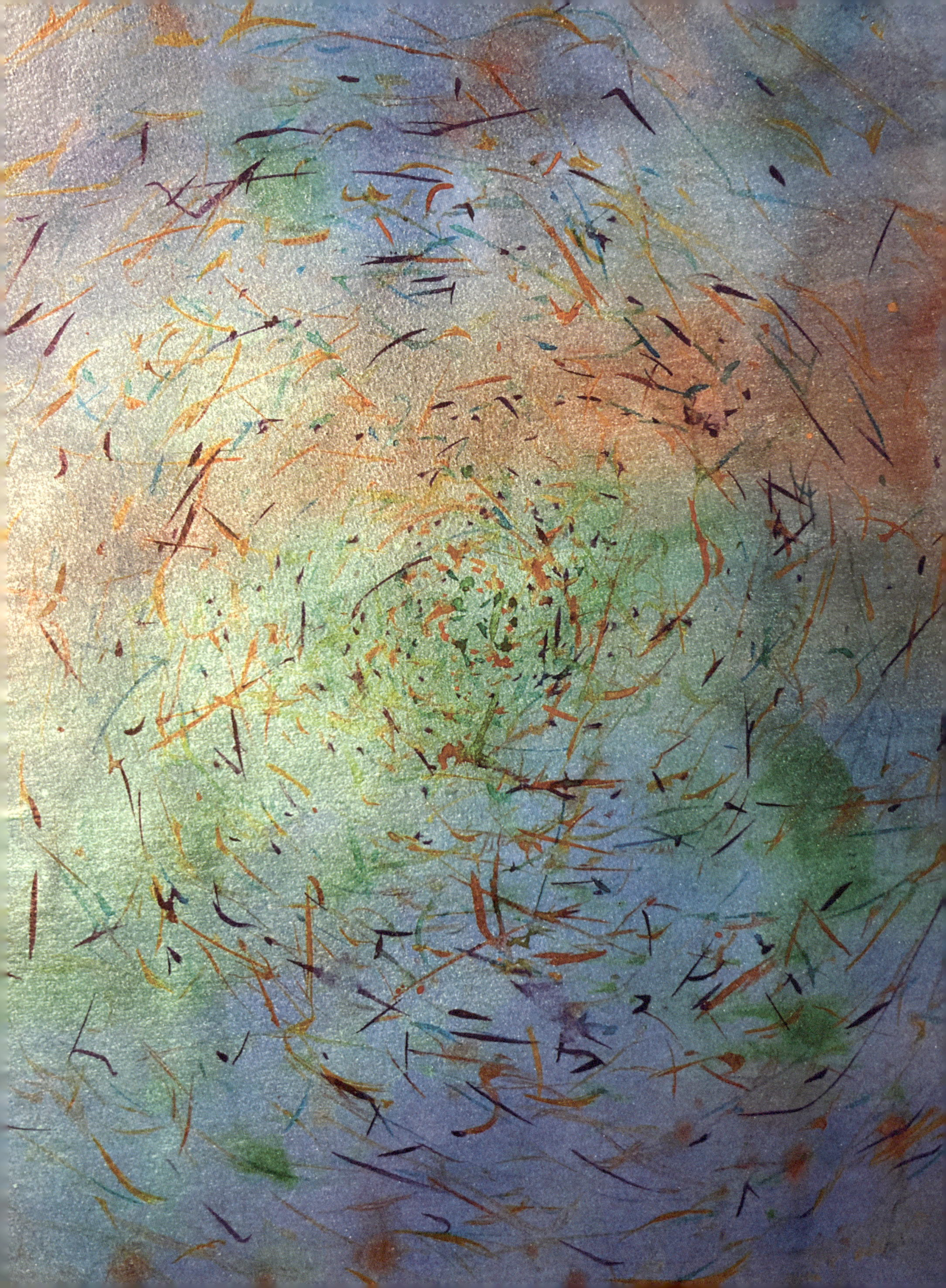

Item 35DI3J: Seven blank books, 1258 CE

It's said that the House of Wisdom, sometimes called the Grand Library of Baghdad, was, by the thirteenth century, the largest library in the world.

It is said that in the preceding centuries the Caliphs poured funds into acquiring and translating texts from Greek, Chinese, Sanskrit, Persian and Latin sages. They preserved and mainlined the knowledge of those civilisations into their own.

It is said that on a midwinter's day in 1258, the knowledge contained within the House of Wisdom reached its peak, then began to decline: the Mongolian army breached the walls at Baghdad and began sacking the city.

The attackers created a bridge across the Tigris by dumping the House of Wisdom's books into the river and riding their horses across.

It's said that the pages bled ink for seven days, staining the river black.

By the eighth day the ink was gone. What remained was a bridge of tens of thousands of blank books.

Our ark contains seven of these blank books.

We say it is worth remembering what has been lost.

◎

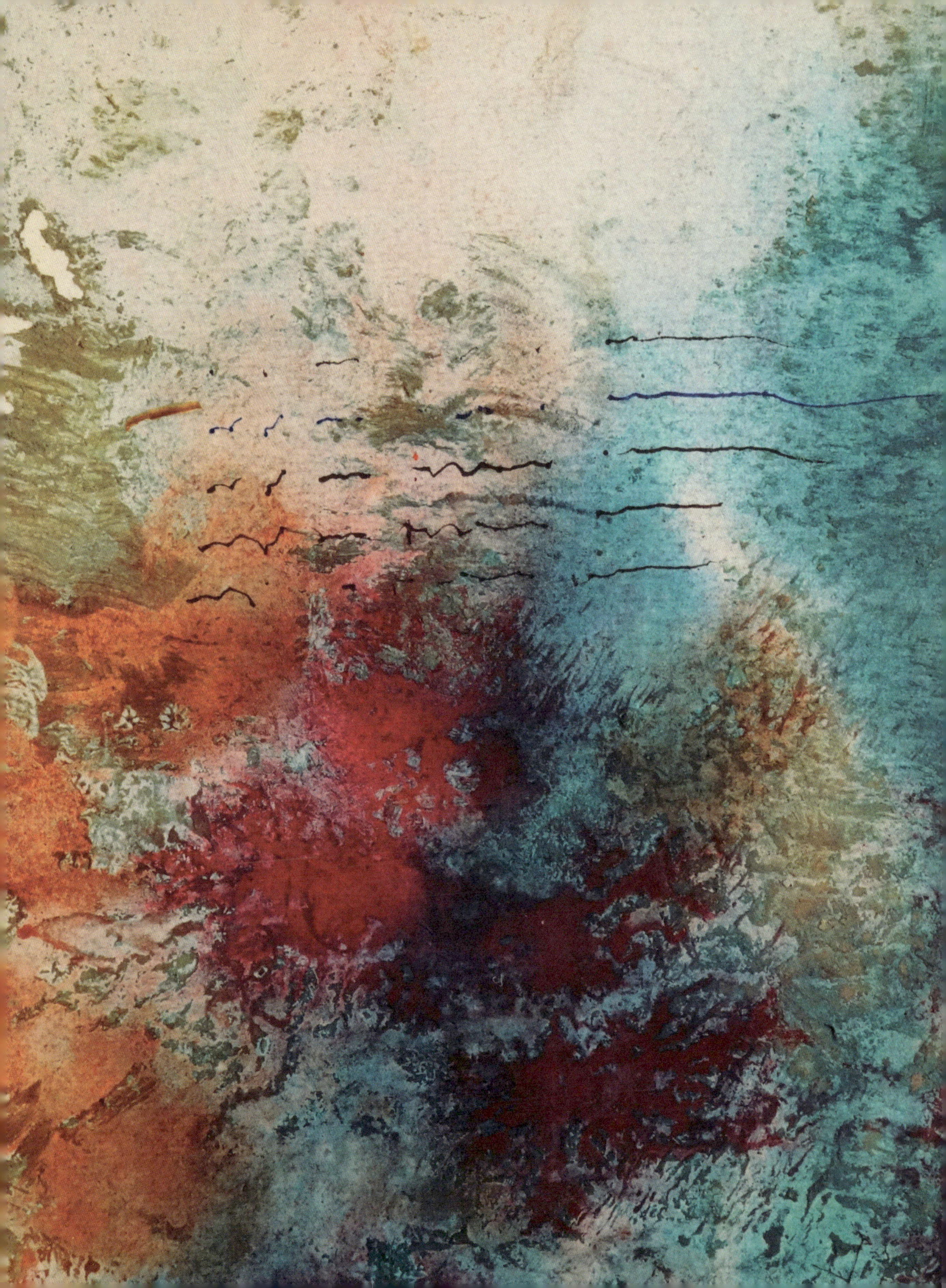

It is said that the Ark of Arks was once carefully catalogued but became scrambled when we scribes began fighting over what should be preserved. Now it is a collection of fragments making only passing sense.

Whole sections are lost. Missing words are noted with --------, though some hypothesise these omissions are deliberate.

It is said that we set out to record lofty truths but quickly descended into banality.

It is said that our loftiest truths are often found in banality.

Do not believe everything people say.

◎

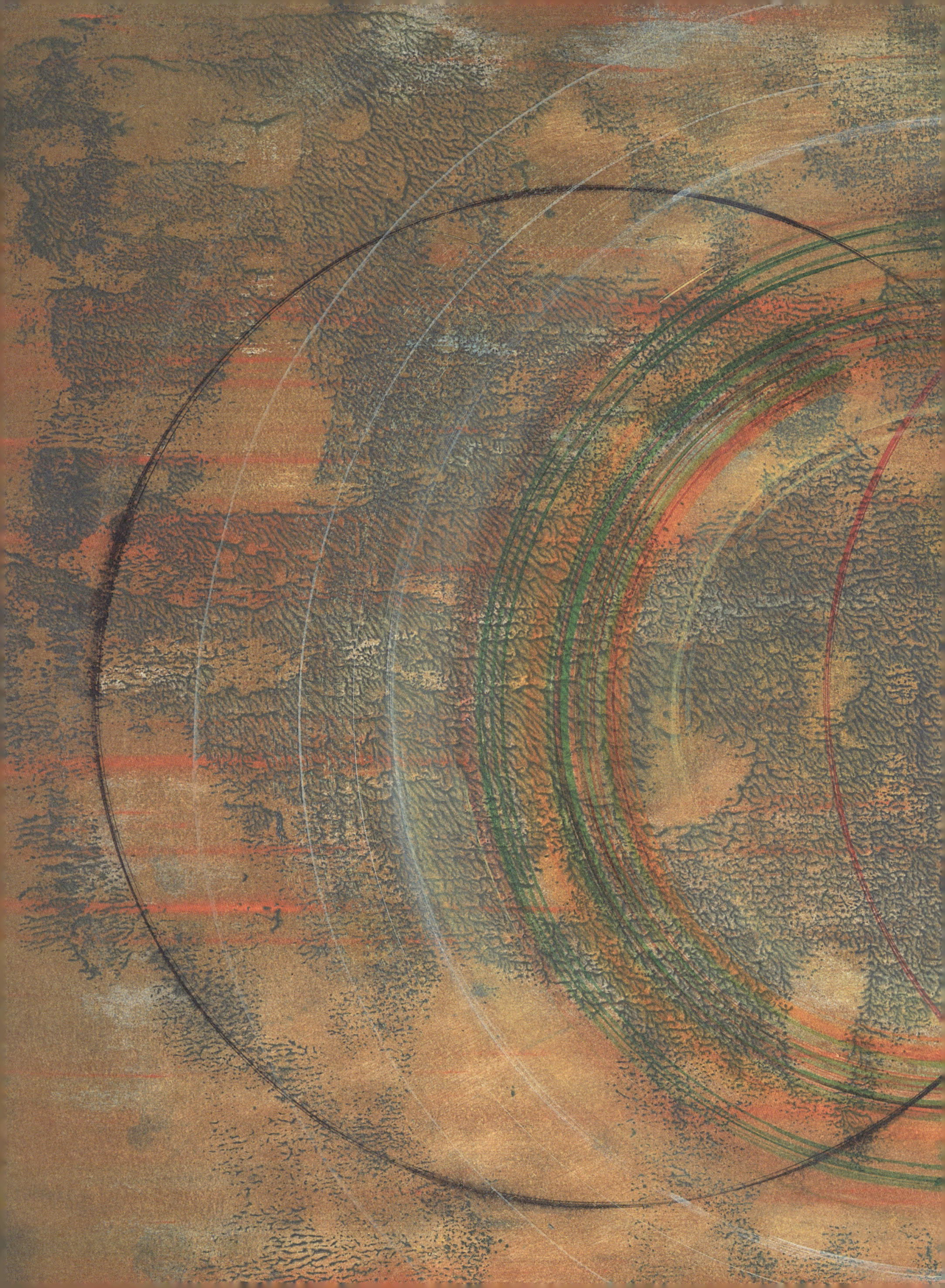

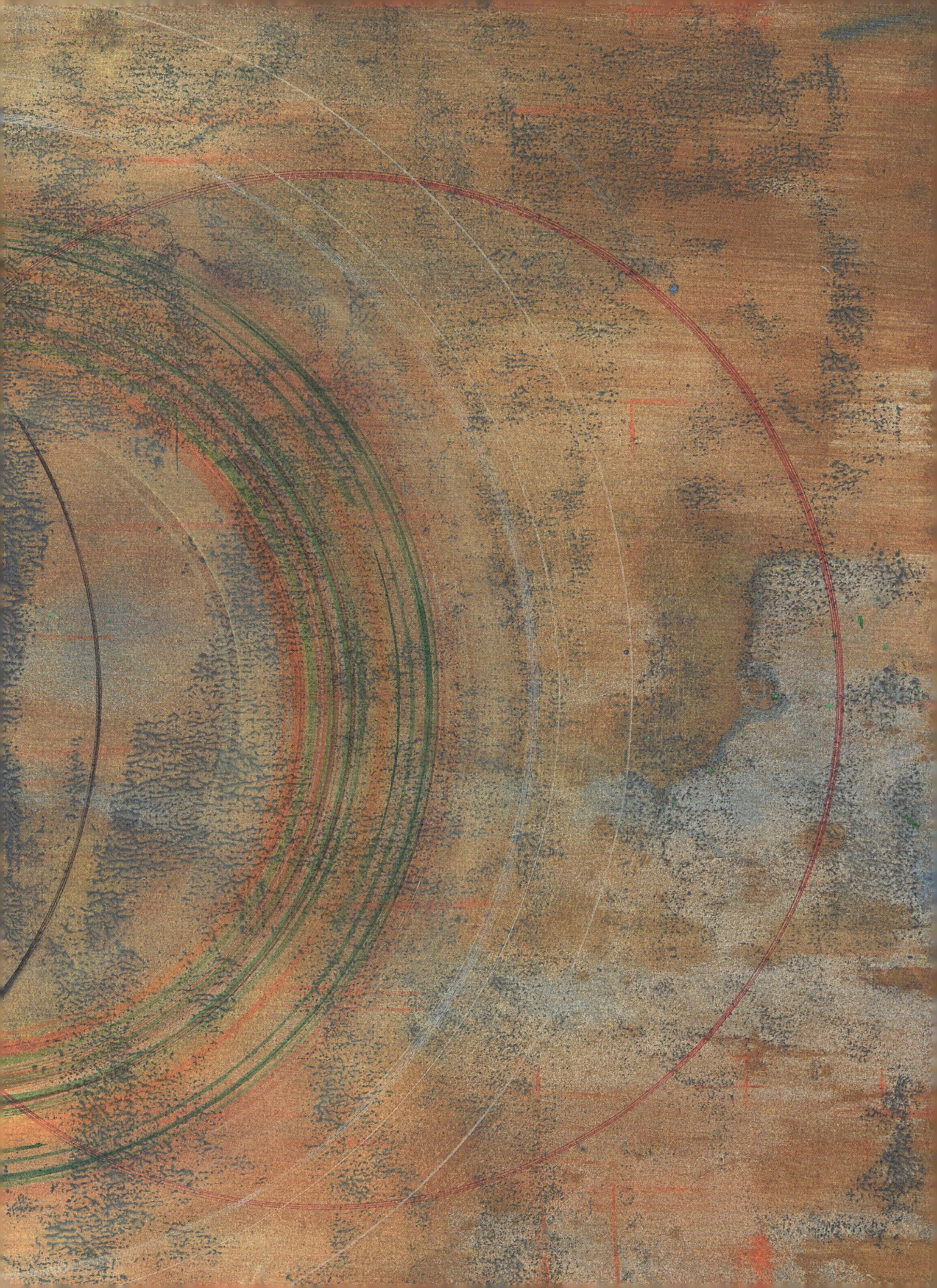

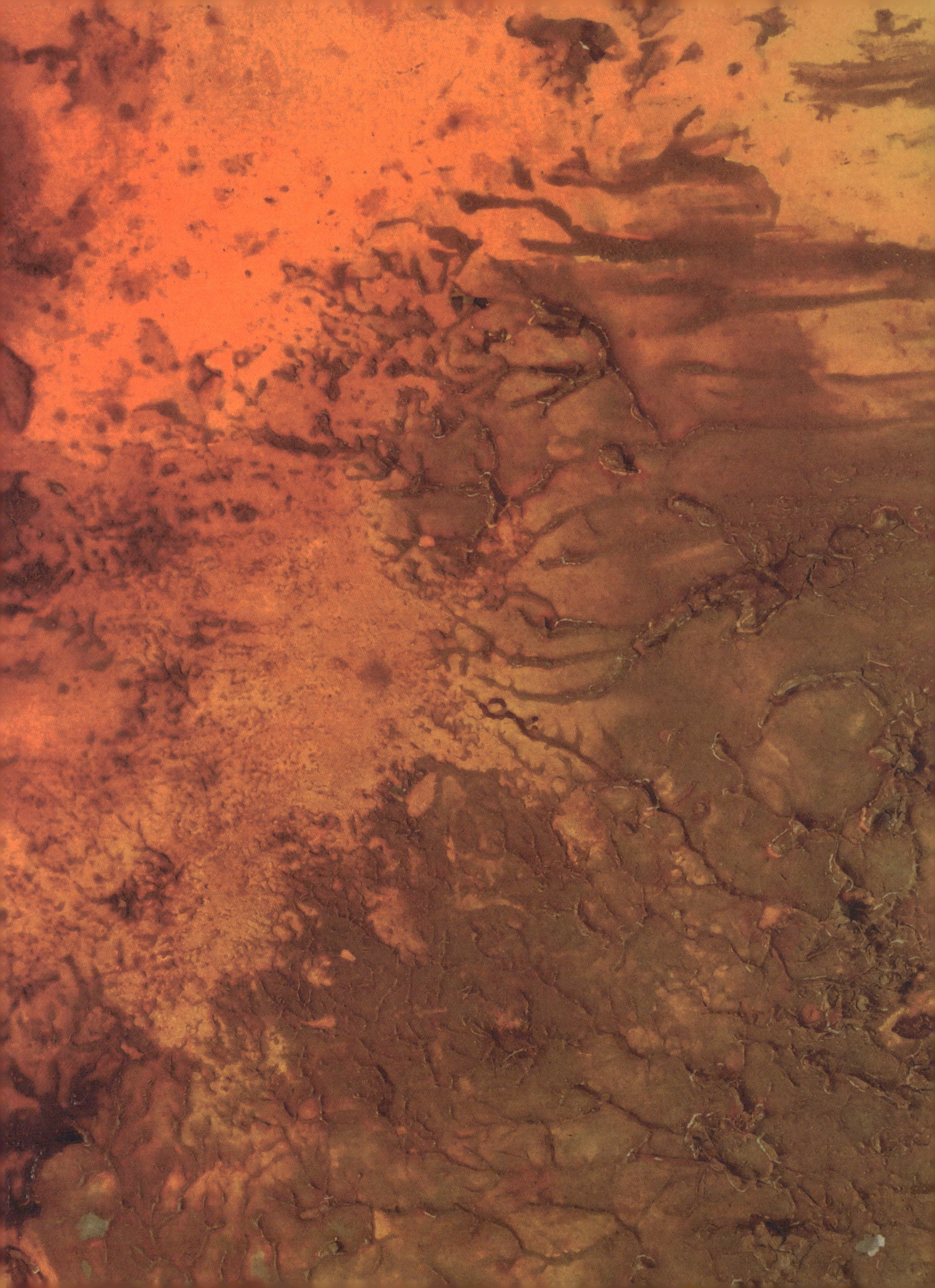

Entry SDFOUF-98008: Epic of Gilgamesh, 2100 BCE

It's said that the Epic of Gilgamesh begins with instructions to examine the foundations of the great walls at Uruk, and there to find a copper tablet box.

You are instructed to take out the secret box, open its bronze lock, take out the tablets of lapis lazuli and read the Epic of Gilgamesh.

The Epic will instruct you to examine the foundations of the great walls at Uruk, and there to find a copper tablet box, and to take out the tablets and begin to read the Epic.

The oldest surviving work of written literature begins by describing a time capsule containing itself.

The oldest work of literature begins with a weird recursive joke.

Time is running out.

◎

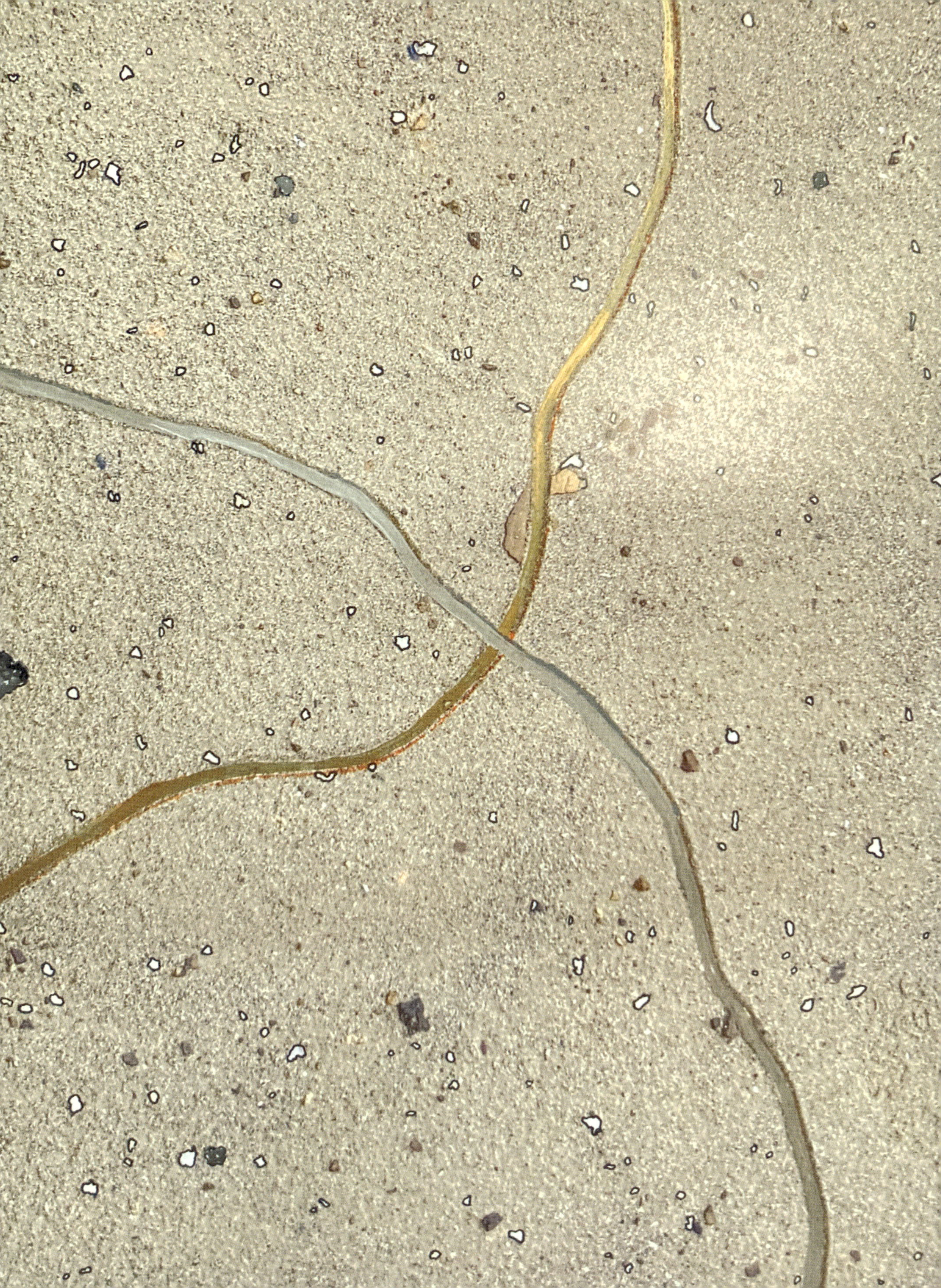

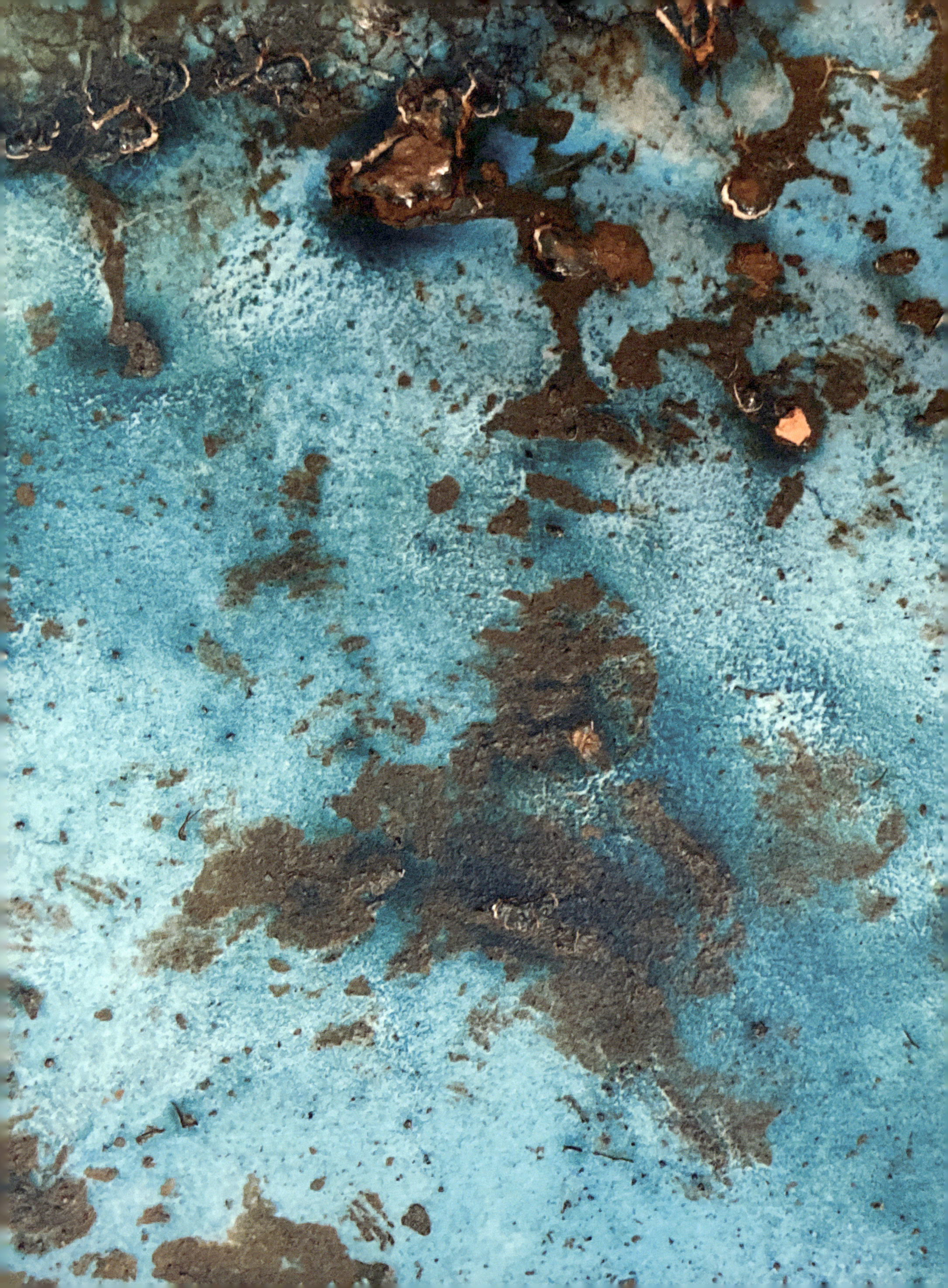

It's true that in the final months we discussed whether we should collect more than the records of other people's arks.

We talked long into the night about how to collect the rivers.

What if Noah had wished to preserve the sea?

We wished to preserve the sea. Our ark must contain that which we must escape.

We talked until dawn about how to collect the wind.

One of our number built wind harps. We spent nights on the beach below the whare at Ōraka listening to his strings mapping the gods.

Harmonics climbed in mathematical shimmers as Hine-pū-nui-o-toka and Hine-rōriki sparred across the sand.

We spent days discussing how to preserve the names of these atua and the stippling they wrought on the dunes.

In takurua we ventured out to film snowflakes describing the patterns of the wind. In raumati we photographed thistledown eddying through the fields beside the whare.

'Ka rere kā pūāwai', the saying goes: thistledown flying, news from afar.

The message: the winds were changing. Old weather patterns were disappearing month by month.

It's said that when our tīpuna first sailed from Hawaiki, trade winds aided their journeys to Aotearoa. When the climate shifted in the fourteenth century, the trade winds changed, closing the migratory corridor.

How many arks set sail but are forced to return?

◎

It's true that in the final months we discussed whether we should collect more than the records of other people's arks.

We talked long into the night about how to collect the rivers.

What if Noah had wished to preserve the sea?

We wished to preserve the sea. Our ark must contain that which we must escape.

We talked until dawn about how to collect the wind.

One of our number built wind harps. We spent nights on the beach below the whare at Ōraka listening to his strings mapping the gods.

Harmonics climbed in mathematical shimmers as Hine-pū-nui-o-toka and Hine-rōriki sparred across the sand.

We spent days discussing how to preserve the names of these atua and the stippling they wrought on the dunes.

In takurua we ventured out to film snowflakes describing the patterns of the wind. In raumati we photographed thistledown eddying through the fields beside the whare.

'Ka rere kā pūāwai', the saying goes: thistledown flying, news from afar.

The message: the winds were changing. Old weather patterns were disappearing month by month.

It's said that when our tīpuna first sailed from Hawaiki, trade winds aided their journeys to Aotearoa. When the climate shifted in the fourteenth century, the trade winds changed, closing the migratory corridor.

How many arks set sail but are forced to return?

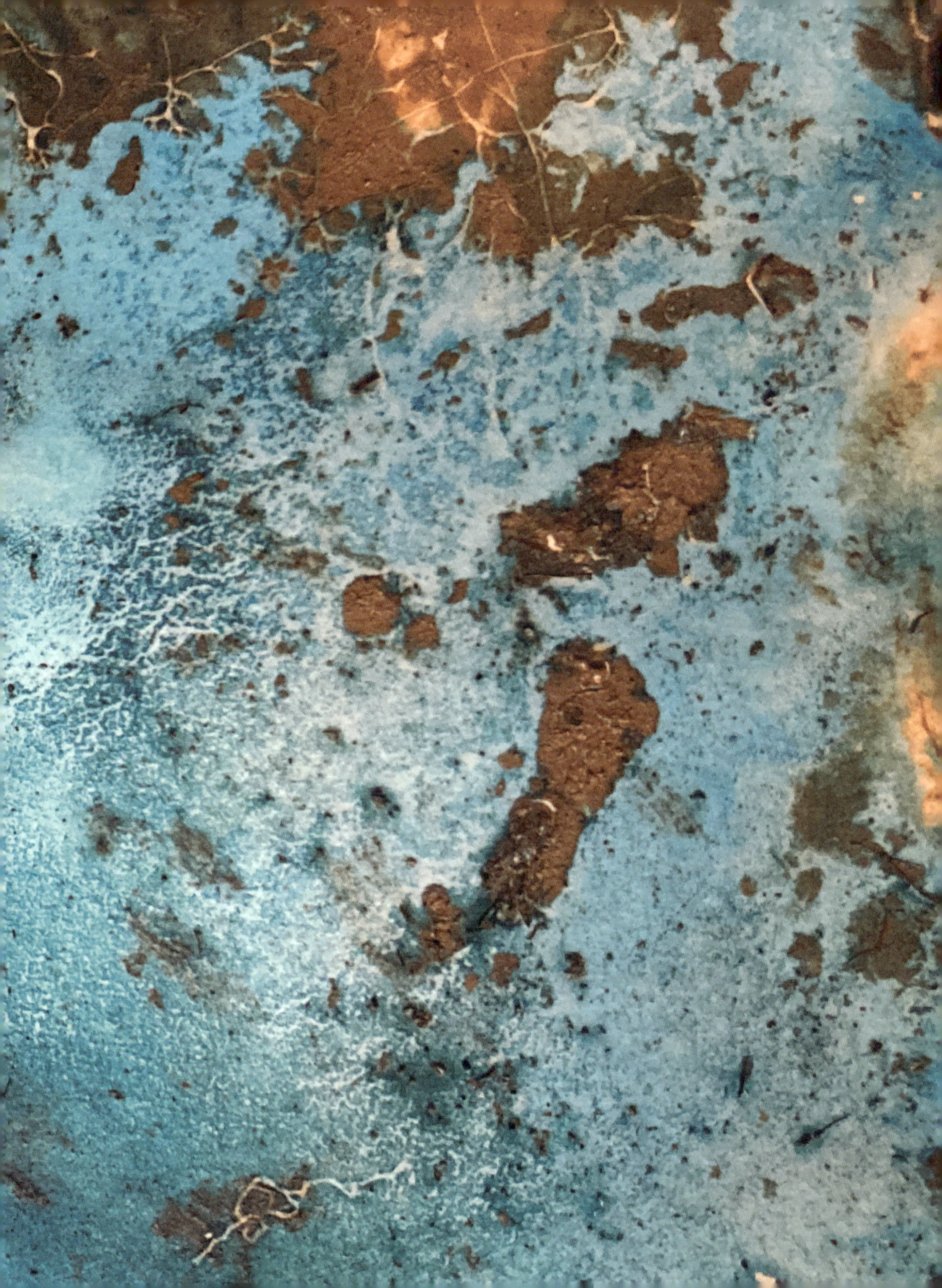

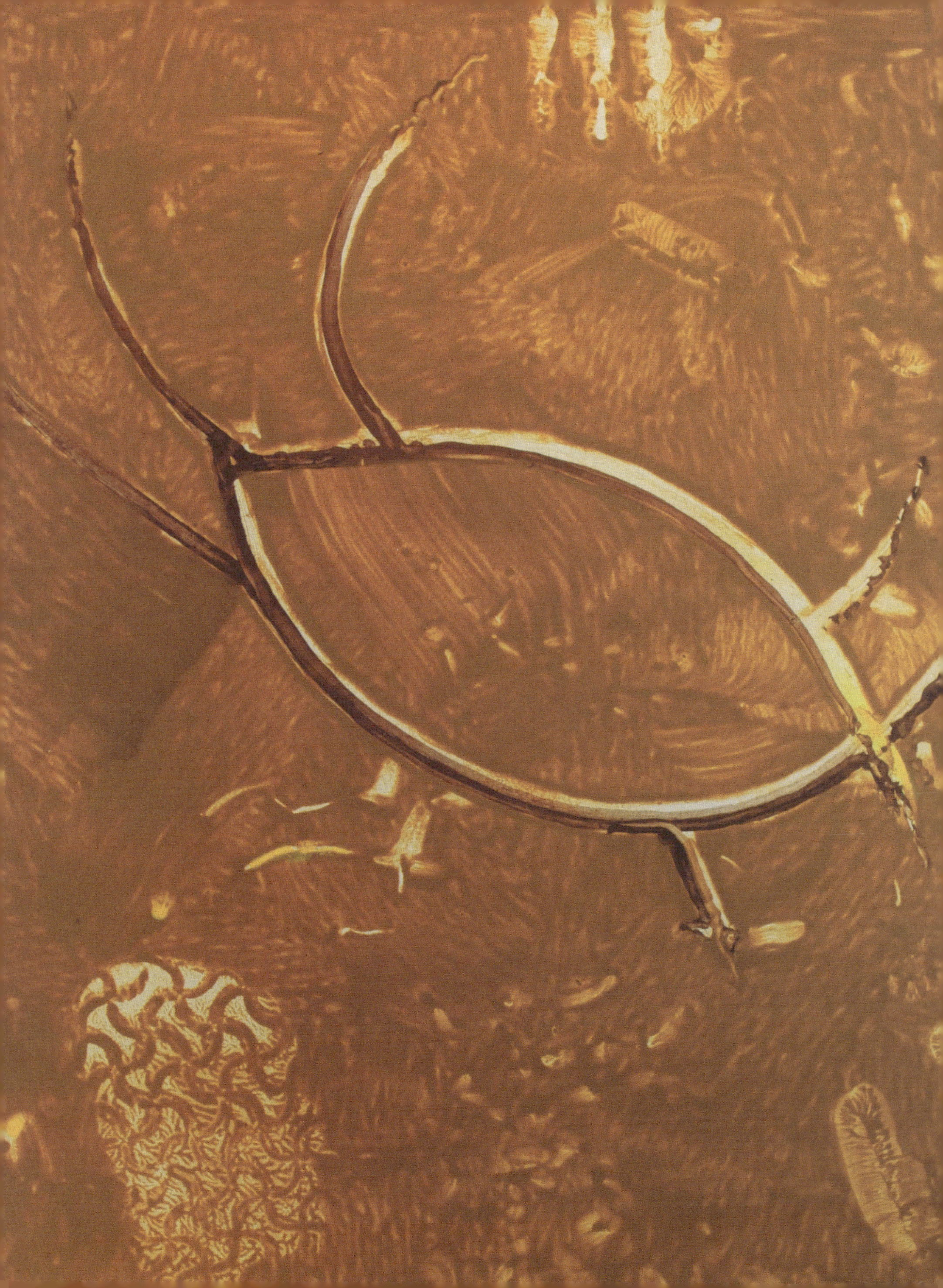

Entry LKJE003033: Svalbard Global Seed Vault, 2008 CE

It's said that high in the Norwegian Arctic, approaching the low rocky island of Spitsbergen, you'll notice among the snow and ice a distant pinprick glow.

It's said that as you draw near, this faint opalescence resolves into a square of gleaming silver and teal. Beneath it a concrete fin juts from the mountainside.

At the fin's base two steel blast doors open onto a corridor tunnelled into the mountain. The corridor terminates in three chambers built to withstand power failure, nuclear blast, meteor strike.

When the power goes out, which it one day will, the surrounding rock and permafrost should keep the chamber steady at –18°C for hundreds of years.

The outer chambers are empty and waiting. Floor-to-ceiling shelves fill the middle chamber. These are stacked with thousands of sealed plastic tubs that hold tens of thousands of foil packets.

Choose one at random. Tear open the foil and pour its tiny jewels into your palm. Plant them and water them and give them light.

The tendrils that shoot will be the envoy of something old, something wild.

It's said that the Svalbard Global Seed Vault holds 13,000 years of agricultural history: over one million varieties of seed.

The many ancestors of wheat. Sacred Cherokee white eagle corn. Ecuadorian carnival squash. The opium poppy's tiny black eyes. Life.

Since the 1990s, the United States has lost 90 per cent of its fruit and vegetable varieties. Almost all rice varieties grown by Chinese farmers in 1950 now exist solely in seed banks. Globally, just thirty crops now account for 95 per cent of the calories humans consume.

It's said that little doomsdays happen daily. Freezers fail. The earth and funding dry up. War destroys scientific institutions and crops.

Hurricane Mitch dispatched Honduras's seed bank. A typhoon left the Philippines's underwater. War damaged Ukraine's in 2022. Thieves destroyed Afghanistan's store of native seeds because they needed the plastic containers.

Svalbard is the remote, off-grid backup centre for the world's 1700 seed banks. It holds the key to feeding us as the climate shifts.

One day Svalbard may hold a sample of every plant on Earth.

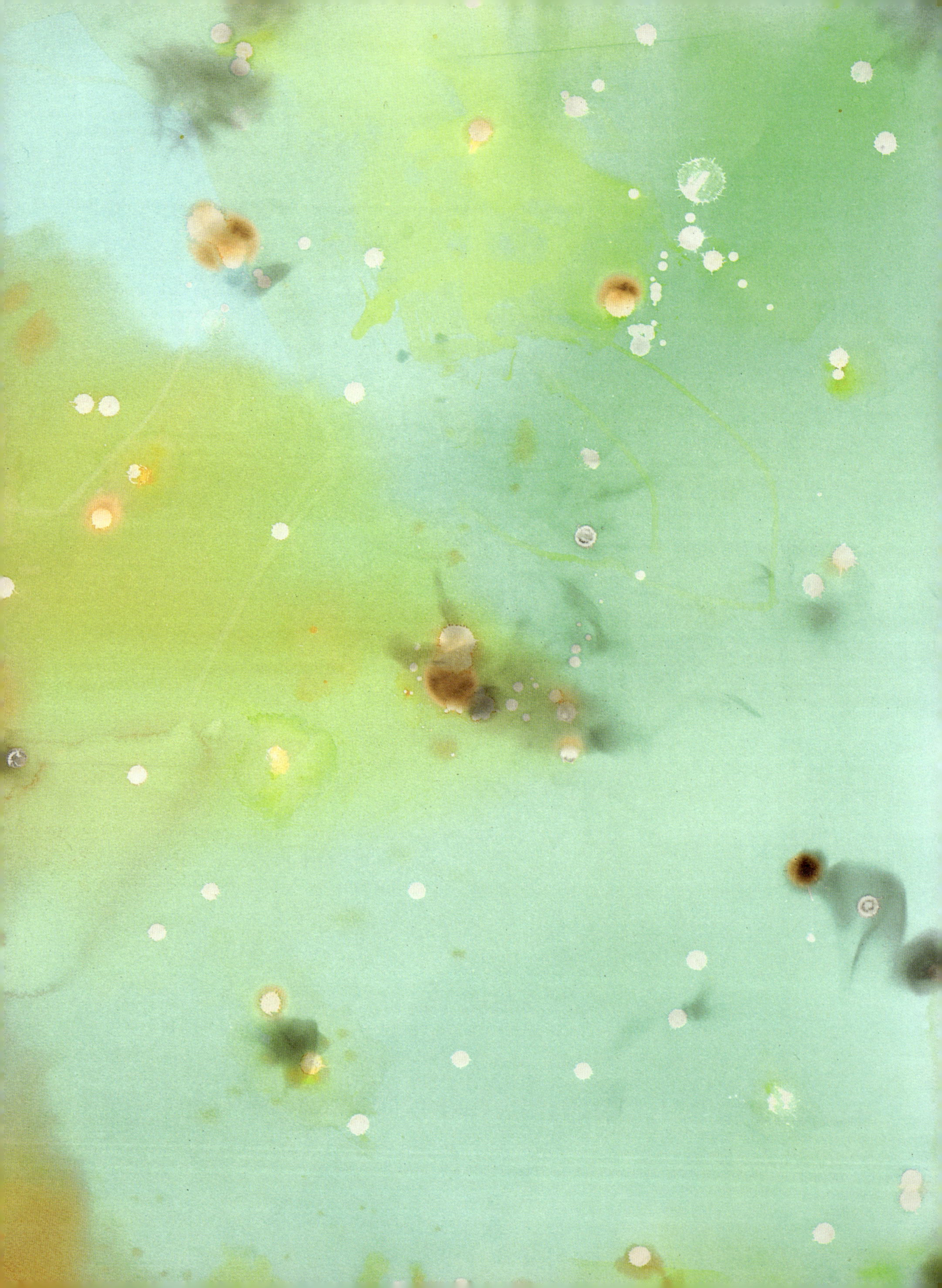

Noah tried to protect his animals from the weather.

We are trying to protect the weather from us.

◎

Waka. Waka huia. Burial ships. Messages in bottles. Arks.

Why vessels that float?

◎

It's said that some of the waka that set sail from Hawaiki to Aotearoa never arrived.

It's said they may still be out there at sea, freighted with ancient knowledges, their crew surviving on fish and microplastics, wheeling slowly off the coast of Hawai'i in the gyre of the great Pacific Garbage Patch.

◎

It is said that we scribes of the whare wānaka first collected documents, images and maps for our Ark of Arks.

It's said that over time some of our number grew suspicious of the representations of things.

We sat wrapped in our cloaks while the rain fell. We watched a bee struggle across the dark sand under bombardment from heavy unseasonal drops.

How could we represent the sound of a bee's microscopic heart? How could we convey the feeling a sated bee has when it lifts from a flower to drift back to the hive?

We argued for weeks about whether to preserve the representation of a thing, or the essence of that thing, or to preserve the thing itself.

It is said we split into three factions. This is mostly correct.

Some of us worked to perfect the art of representation through writing, photographing and filming.

Some of us began collecting the things we had once described. We collected bees, and hives. Seeds and specimens of the trees and plants of Aotearoa, native and introduced. We began buying up the material remnants of other arks. Through our agents we bought treasures at auctions worldwide. Several times a week container trucks rumbled through our gates.

And some of us began meditating upon the essence of each object we wished to preserve. We recorded the principles and virtues of these things, taking care not to reference the thing itself, and stored these records and destroyed the things.

None of us went mad.

◎

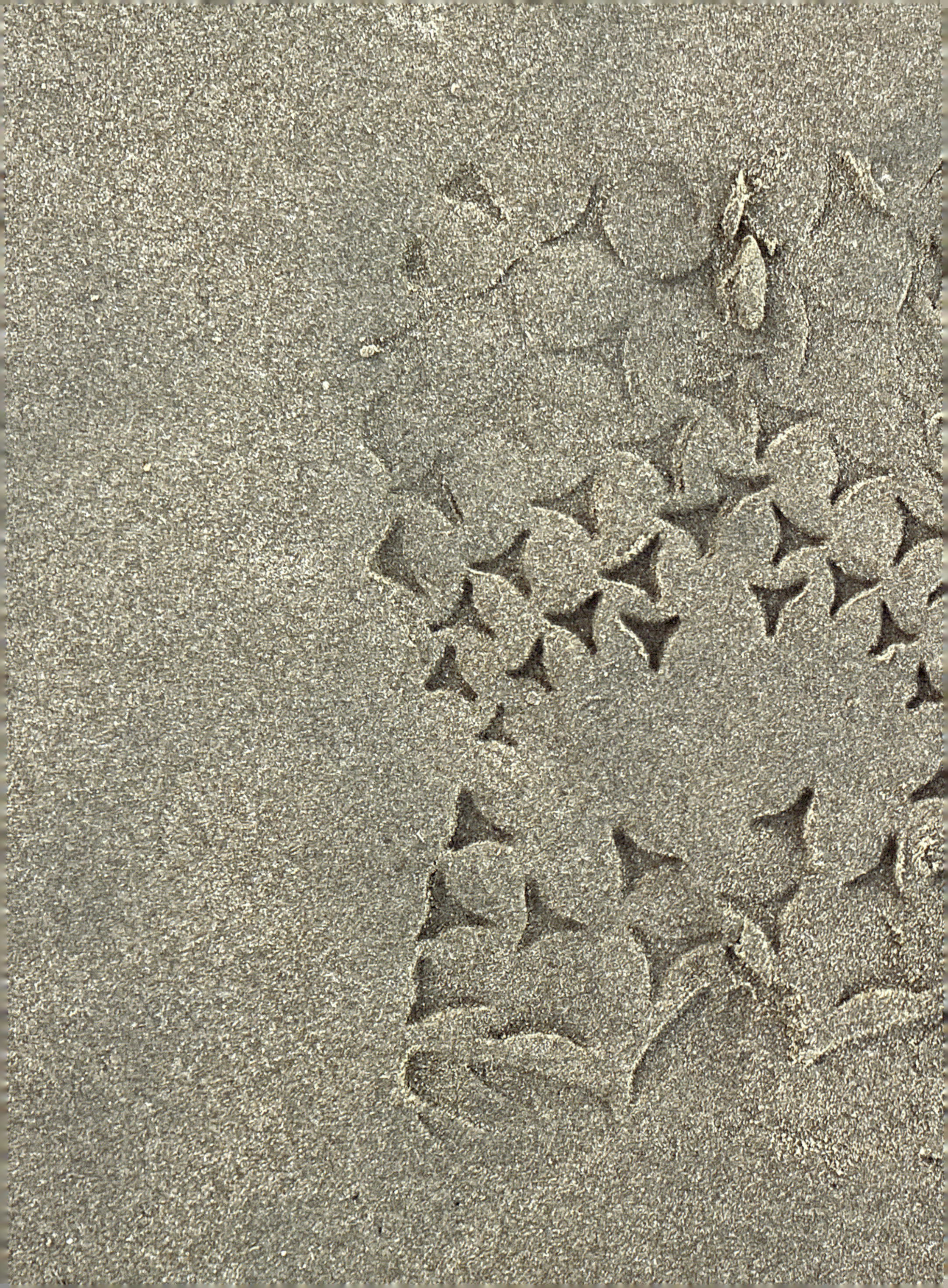

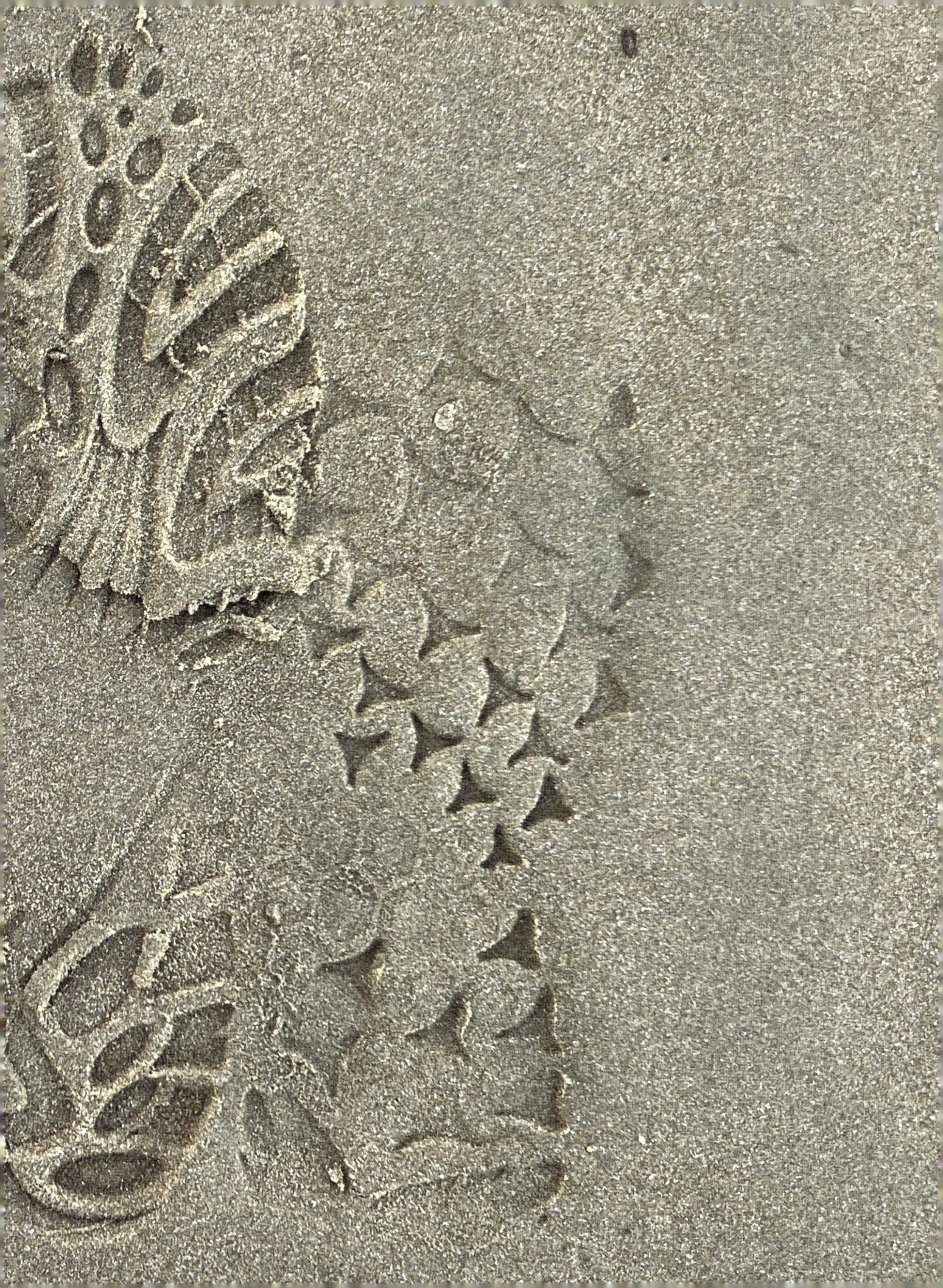

Item 08FDS08S-SF808F: Icarda Dry Area Crop Store, 2012 CE

They say that Aleppo — today a metropolis bounded by olive groves, then the terminus of the Silk Road — is among the oldest continuously inhabited cities in the world.

Take a shovel to the cobbles of Mousslama Ben Abdel Malek Street, outside the butcher's that sits across from Al Sultaniyeh Mosque, and you'll unearth an earthen time capsule demonstrating how different civilisations will love the same place.

Dig down through the sediment of memory that is a city, past the fractured bones of modern Syria to those of the French, the Ottomans and Mongols, down through the early Islamic, Roman, Byzantine and Seleucid folk, to -------- nomads who camped nearby 11,000 years ago.

It's said that up on the dusty rise above you, where Aleppo's citadel now stands in late-afternoon sun, old Abraham, patriarch of patriarchs, used to milk his sheep.

It's said that the stone fortress there is the only ancient fortification to be used in a modern war.

Inside, the Syrian Army dug in. Outside, Free Syrian Army batteries thumped and bucked all night. Snipers killed rebel soldiers and stray dogs.

It's said that away to the south-west the shelling cracked the plaster on the walls of the International Centre for Agricultural Research in the Dry Areas (ICARDA). Lights flickered. The power came and went. The scientific staff evacuated to Beirut.

They left behind tens of thousands of samples in the centre's seed bank: the wild matriarchs of today's crops, gathered from the valleys and plains where the domestication of crops began.

All were adapted to the driest, harshest places on --------, where our ancestors lived, and where our descendants will too.

It's said that as air strikes pushed the Free Syrian Army back across the city, one of their patrol units, mostly teenagers, some of them cousins, took refuge in the abandoned ICARDA compound. They ransacked the place, looking for weapons, valuables, food. They found none.

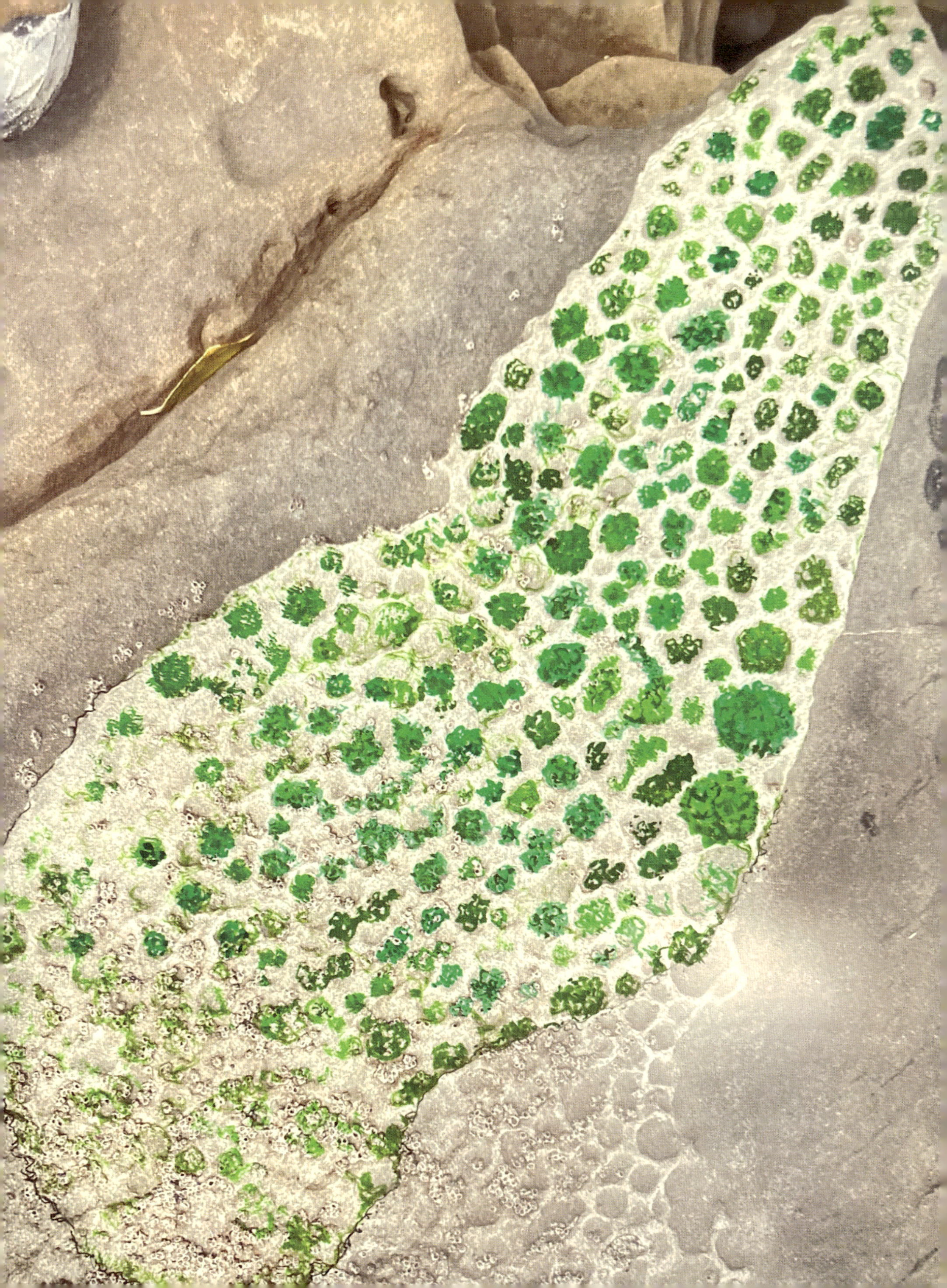

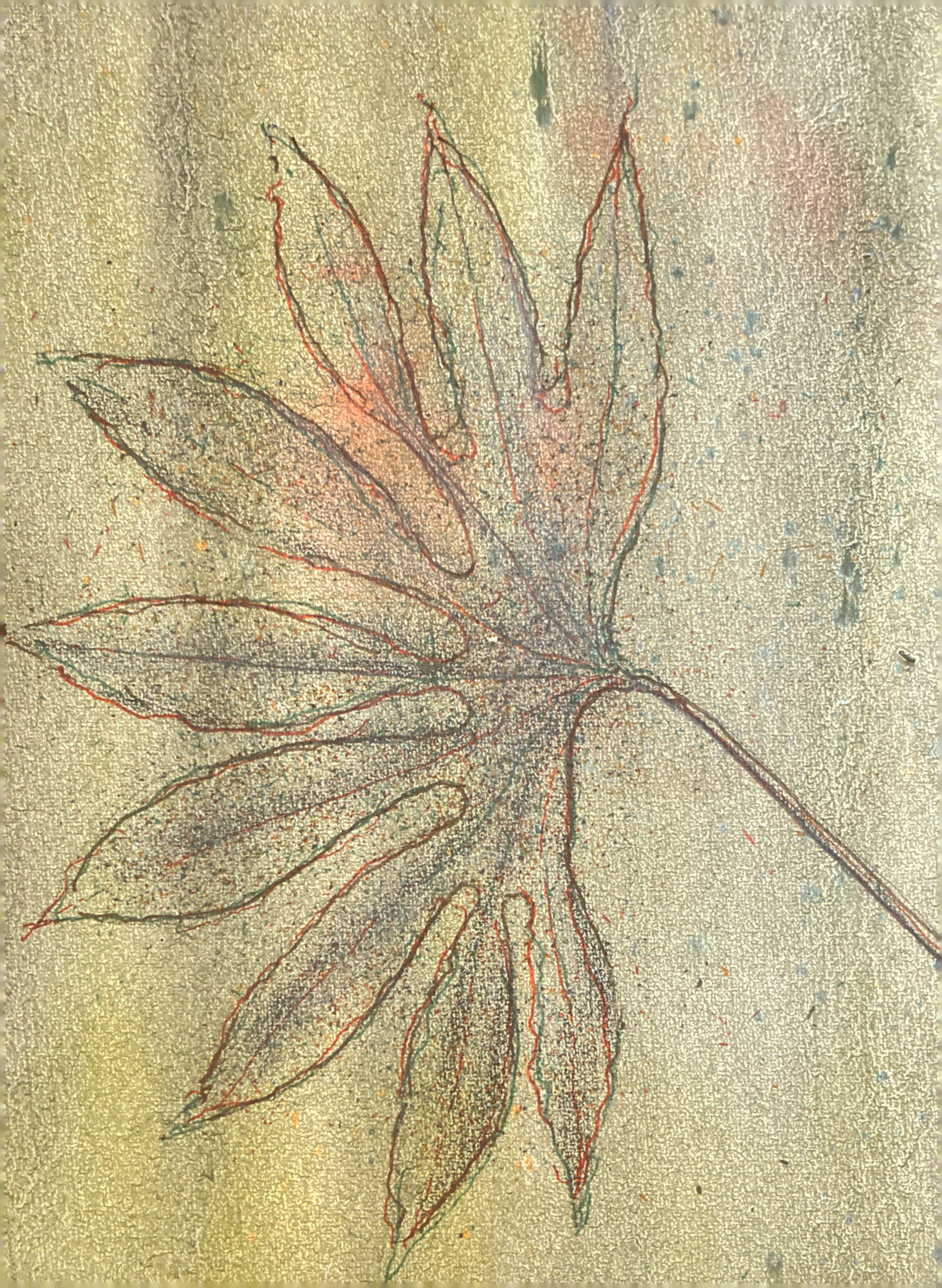

It's said that Russian air strikes kept them pinned down inside the building for a week. With their rations depleted, the sergeant led a breakout from the back door where, three steps down the laneway, beneath graffiti that translated, mysteriously, as 'this is happiness', he took a sniper's bullet in the thigh.

They retreated into the compound. They began to look differently at the grains stored inside.

On dusk, in the courtyard at the back of the building, where the ICARDA support staff used to gossip and smoke, the soldiers lit a small fire and cooked up a bowl of strange, bitter-tasting chickpeas.

It was a flavour well known to the people of the Nile Valley — in the time of the pharaohs — that would, once the youngest among them licked his plate clean, be extinct.

◎

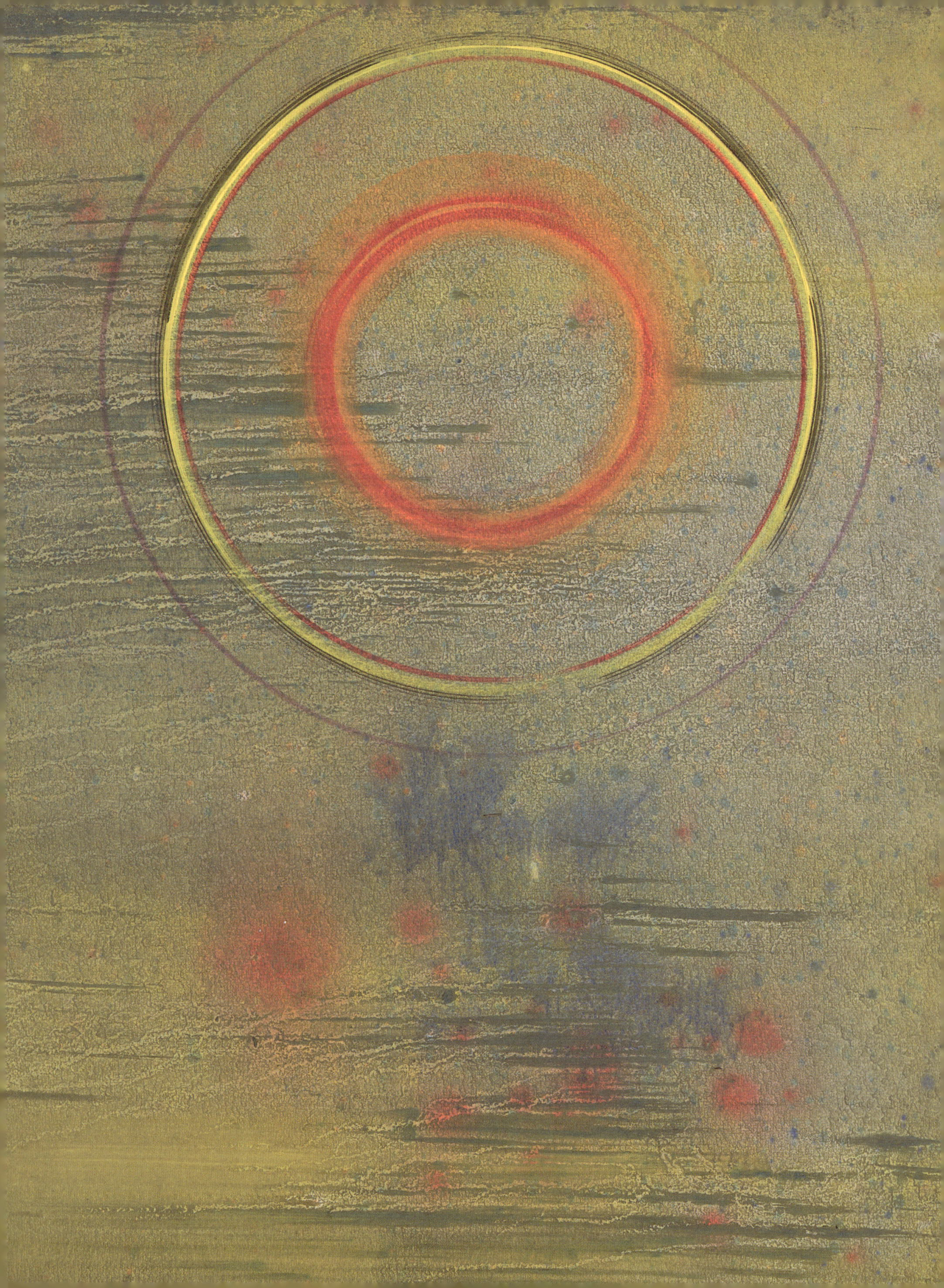

Item DSC8-00F8D: Hinu Moa, 184- CE

It's said that the Ngāi Tahu men who guided Crown agent Walter Mantell down the east coast of Te Waipounamu were not playing a practical joke when they chose to camp at --------.

With its rill of fresh water down the beach, a wall of sheltering dunes and abundant kai from estuary, river mouth and sea, the nohoaka there had been used for centuries on the coastal journey.

It's said that when the men made camp and chose a spot to dig their umu, they were surprised to unearth a ring of blackened boulders, hefty bones, and shell fragments from large eggs.

Weary from the day's march, they lit a fire in the old umu, set their fish down to cook and sealed it with earth.

When they began to eat, first one fell silent, then all. They exchanged looks by the queer light of their fire.

The kai tasted otherworldly. Oily and rich and dark, infused with a heavy smokiness that could only be the fat of the long-extinct moa.

They were the first to taste moa in centuries.

It began to rain, heavy drops hitting the sand.

-------- spoke first.

--------, he said, and the others collapsed in the sand from laughing so hard.

It's said that night a group of women filled the men's dreams. They wore unfamiliar moko kauae on their chins, and spoke and laughed in a language that was not their own.

◎

It's said that the ICARDA team knew of the Svalbard Global Seed Vault long before fighting threatened Aleppo.

It's said that before hungry teenagers ate the institute's stores, their scientists had shipped samples of their seeds to the frozen north.

In 2015 the ICARDA team made the first withdrawal from Svalbard's vault.

When the shipment arrived at their new headquarters in Tehran, the Syrian scientists were reverent as they sliced open the boxes and seed packets and thumbed each seed into dark soil.

Small green shoots came up. As small green shoots do.

No one could say whether the young soldiers, later interred in shallow graves at the back of the ICARDA courtyard, were seeds.

◎

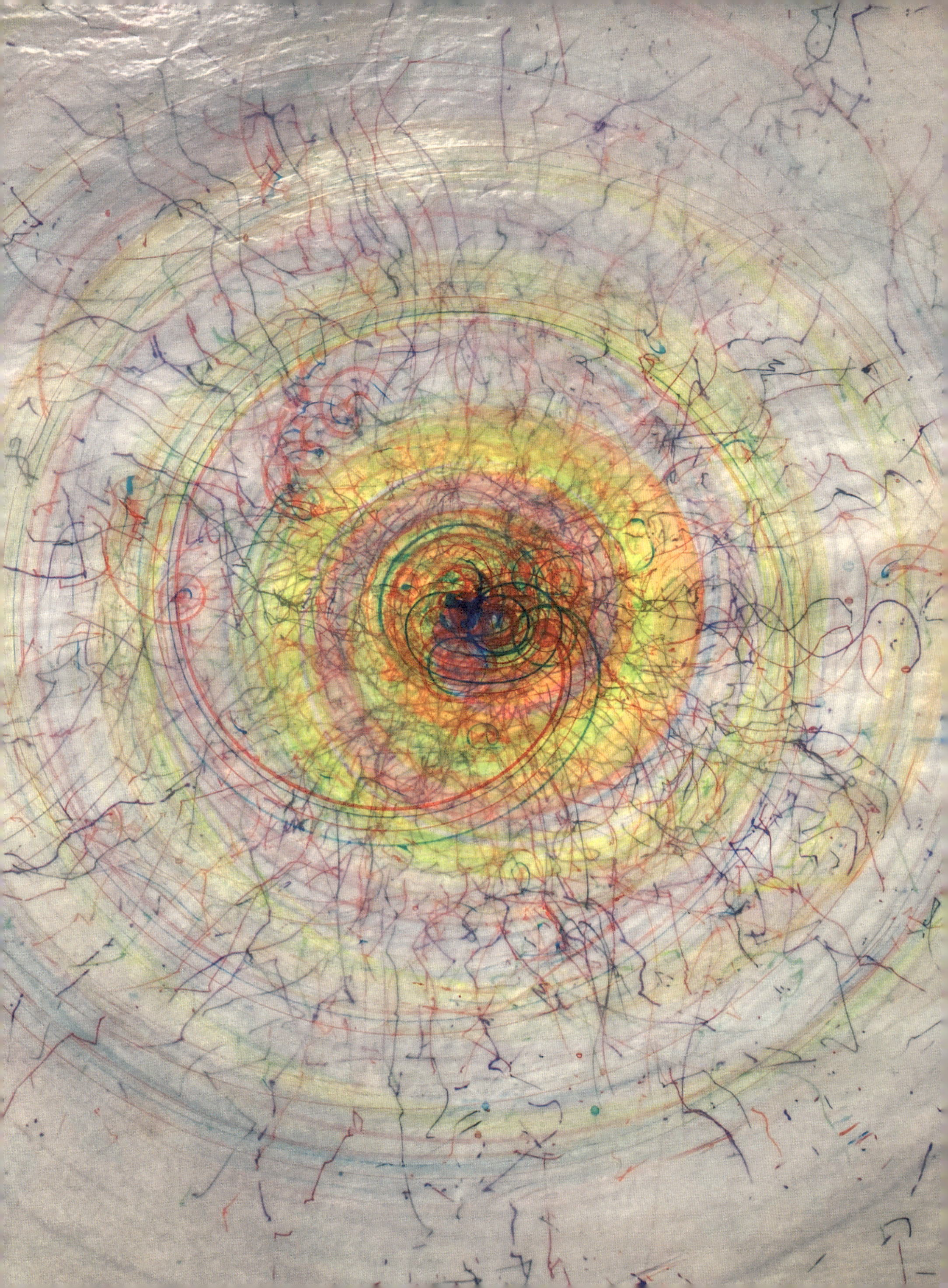

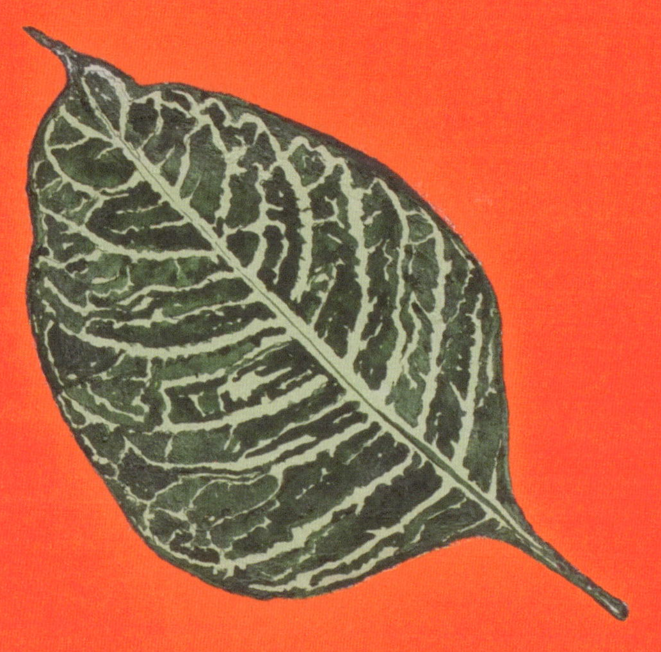

Item 0498DJJJDZ: Svalbard Global Seed Vault, 2017 CE

The Svalbard ark was said to be failsafe. Even without power, the seeds within would be preserved by arctic permafrost.

It's said that in 2016 temperatures on Spitsbergen ran 7° warmer than the long-term average.

In 2017 the permafrost surrounding the vault melted for the first time. The access tunnel flooded, then later refroze into a block of ice.

It's said that no seeds were lost. It's said they installed pumps.

'Semi-permafrost' is not yet a word.

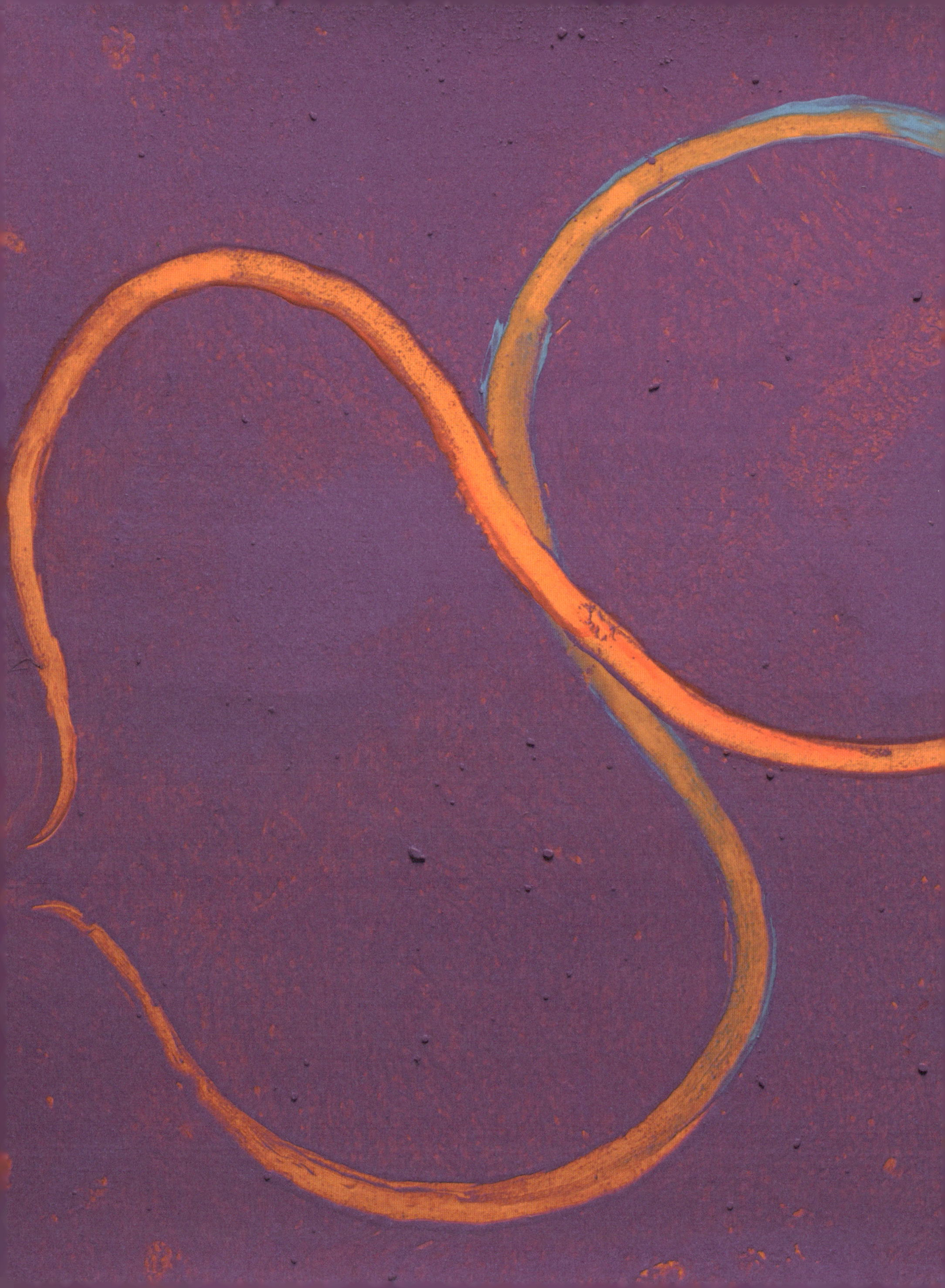

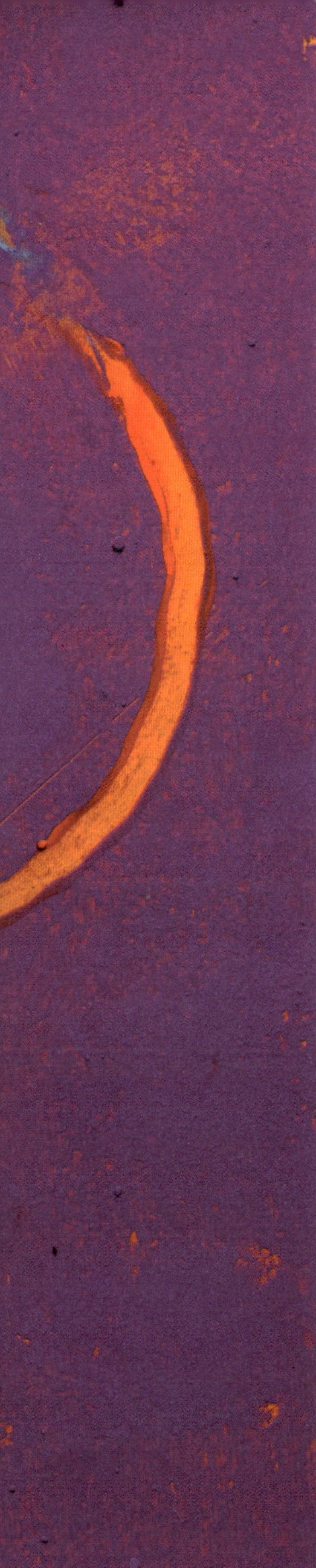

Item 230984DF0S8FDS0: Record of love, 197- CE

It's said that in the late '70s, after years spent working together as colleagues and friends, two Americans fell for each other. They created a time capsule from the early moments of their love.

The couple chose a selection of stirring music and a recording of the woman's brainwaves while she meditated upon the feeling of love.

These vibrations, musical and electromagnetic, were cut to two records. These records were then attached to two rockets and fired into space.

In today's currency, the project cost close to $5 billion.

The woman was Ann Druyan, creative director of the Voyager Interstellar Message Project. The man was astronomer Carl Sagan.

When the world ends with the collapse of our sun, those golden records affixed to Voyager I and II may be the only remaining trace of who we were.

The probes will be long dead, transformed from scientific instruments to time capsules; to fossils buried in space.

It's said that if extra-terrestrial life finds the Voyager probes, it will be intrigued by technology like the atomic batteries that power the craft.

We say that language was the most advanced technology on board.

It's said that the key impulse behind the missions was scientific discovery.

Some among us believe the key impulse was to share the feeling of new love with the void.

It is said that an ark is an admission that the worst has happened, and that destiny cannot be reversed. To build an ark is to throw the future you believed in to the wolves. You must leave everything behind and cast off.

It's said that an ark is a gesture of hope in the future. Pushing your boat out into a dark sea creates the opposite shore.

It's said that the hardest part is deciding who to leave behind.

It's said that on the first voyaging canoes from Hawaiki, the tohuka chanted karakia invoking islands beyond the horizon as fish to be reeled in towards the boat.

It's said that those of us fascinated by apocalypse entertain a fantasy of our own virtue: we never imagine being left behind.

It's said that those of us fascinated by apocalypse have a secret desire to leave everything behind.

The more our Ark of Arks accurately captured our world, the more we were seized by homesickness and grief for a place we had not yet left.

◎

It's said that if Noah launched his ark today, he and his animals would be intercepted by the Australian Defence Force and towed to an offshore processing facility. The animals would be homed. Noah would be held in indefinite detention.

It's said that today we respond to the threat of floods by criminalising arks.

◎

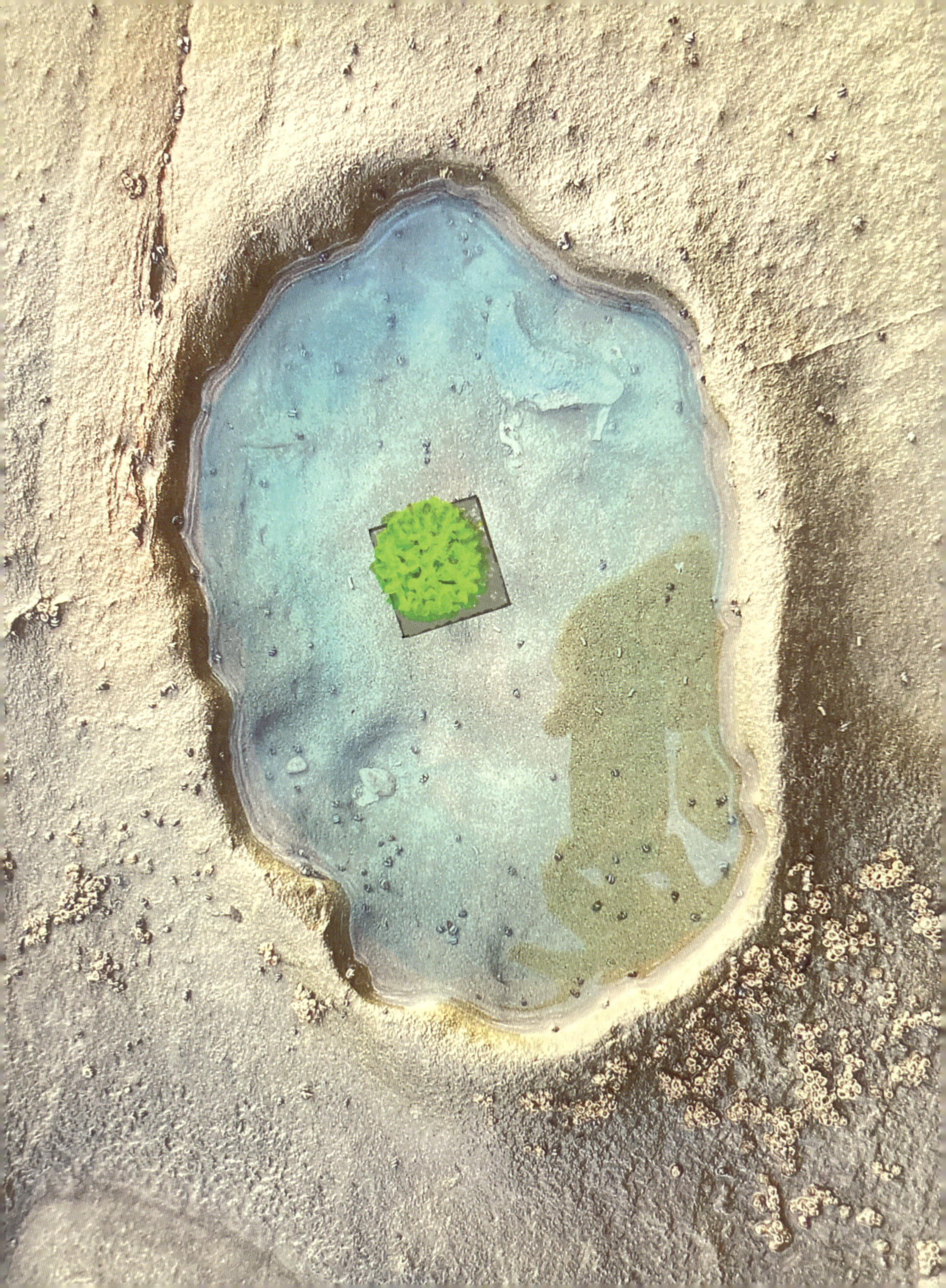

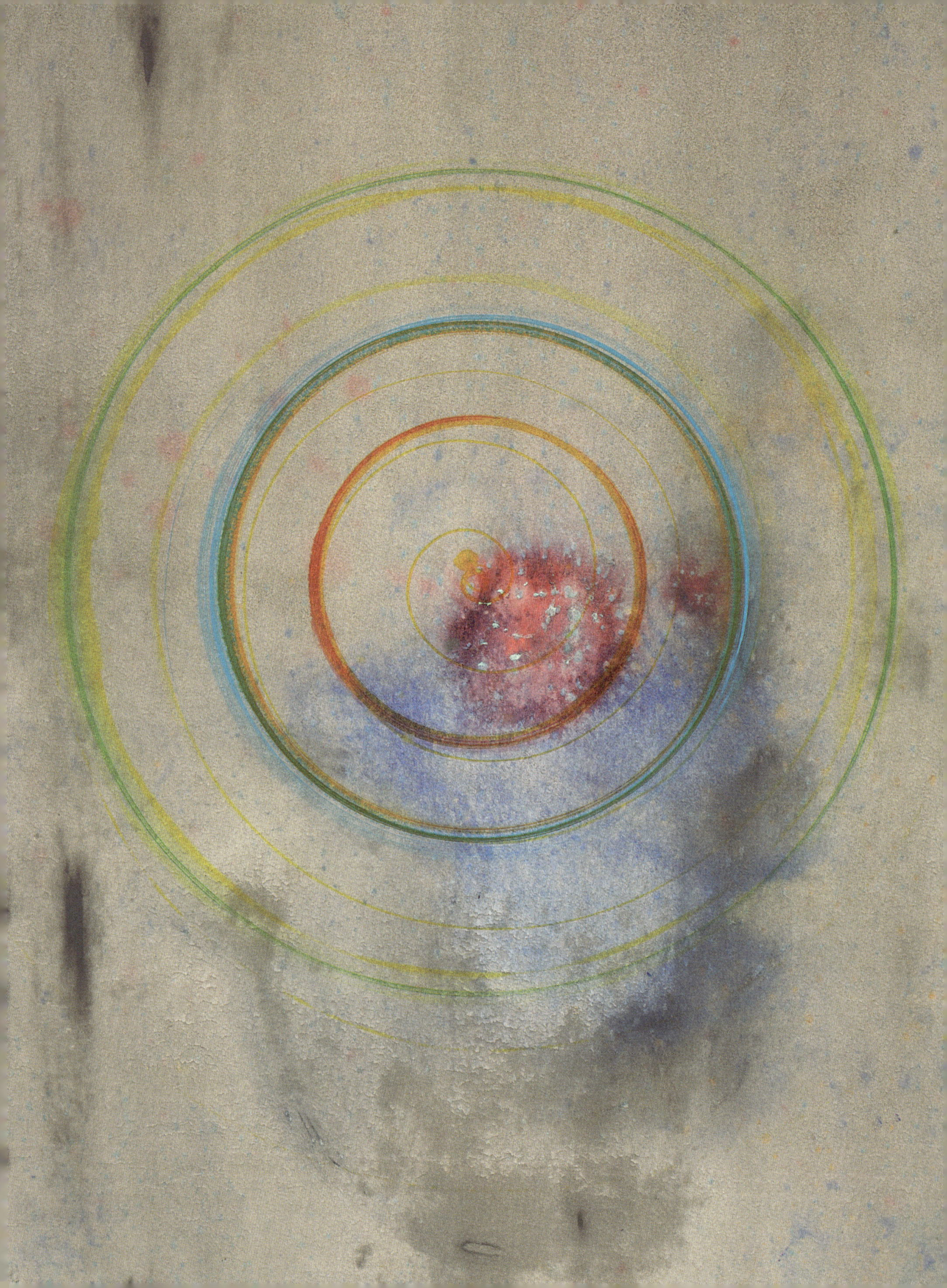

It's said that in the dry, tawny schist country of inland Ōtākou, the rough lichened stone erodes to form shelters and clefts that make excellent natural hiding places.

It's said that if you know where to look you will find a finely woven kete containing a cloakmaker's tools: bone needles, carefully bound bundles of moa feathers, skeins of muka.

It's said that the old people still intend to come back for these things.

In those arid hills, nothing lasts longer than it should.

◎

It is said the world's museums contain hundreds of millions of artefacts from all known civilisations.

Each day, nearly all of those taoka go unseen and forgotten by the living. On average 5 per cent are on display.

The rest sleep.

◎

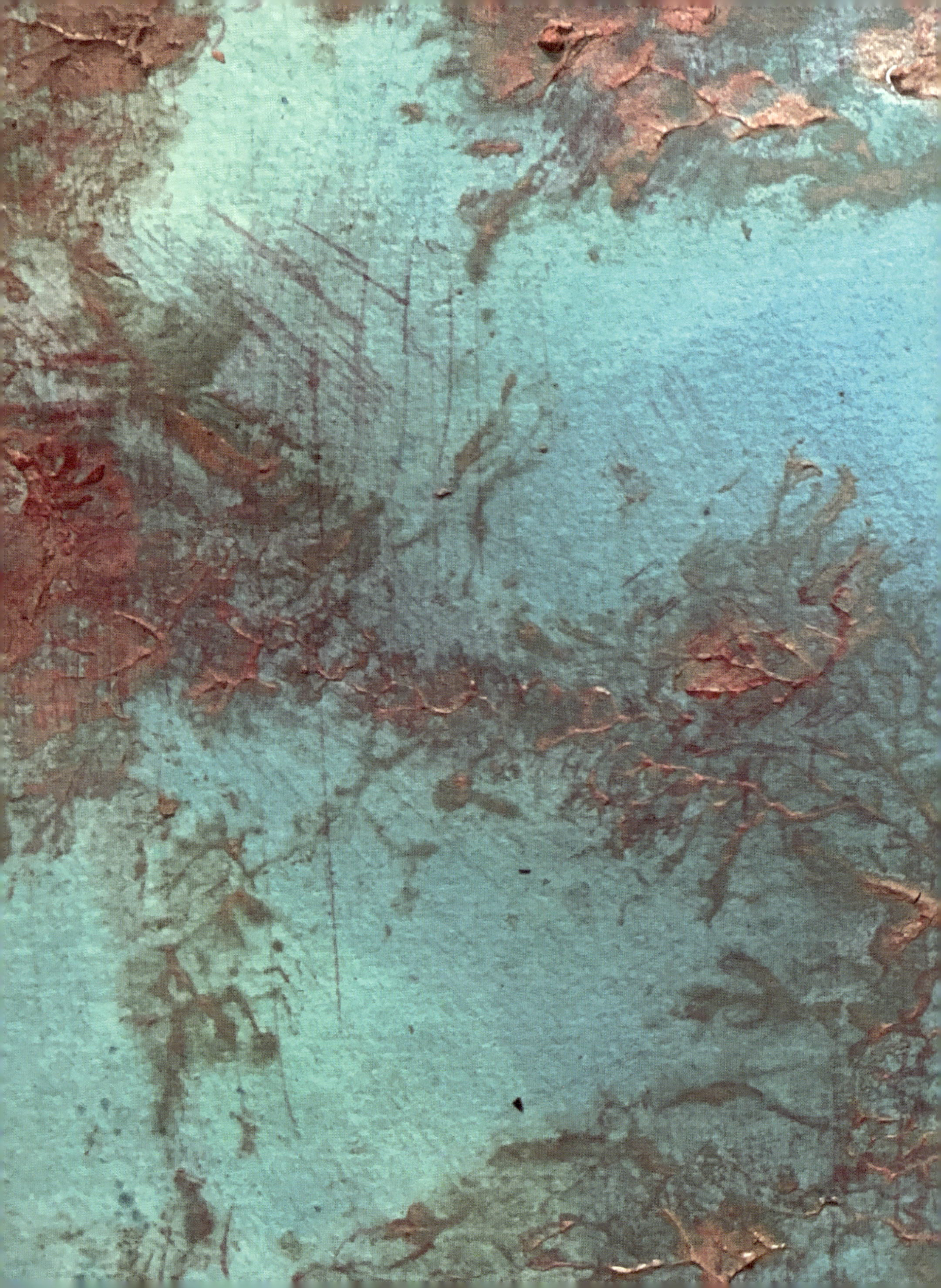

Entry DFLKJ0022110: First arrivals I, 11-- CE

We say that when our tīpuna beached the twin hulls of their voyaging waka on Aotearoa's shores, and their arrival karakia faded to birdsong and the people took sea-leg steps onto the hard, wet sand at --------, they set about converting an ark back into a world.

We say they unloaded all conversations, all laughter, all debate, all questions, all ways of loving, all whakapapa, all jokes, all schools of thought, all kūmara and kūmara rites, all animosity, all arts, all star paths, all curiosity, all gods, all feuds, all karakia, all seeds, all tools, all methods of war, all rites of birth, all knowledges pertaining to thriving in an unknown land.

We consider these old people our grandparents and remember them with love.

We say that we, their descendants, are living proof that arks work.

◎

Entry DFLKJ0022110: First arrivals I, 11-- CE

We say that when our tīpuna beached the twin hulls of their voyaging waka on Aotearoa's shores, and their arrival karakia faded to birdsong and the people took sea-leg steps onto the hard, wet sand at --------, they set about converting an ark back into a world.

We say they unloaded all conversations, all laughter, all debate, all questions, all ways of loving, all whakapapa, all jokes, all schools of thought, all kūmara and kūmara rites, all animosity, all arts, all star paths, all curiosity, all gods, all feuds, all karakia, all seeds, all tools, all methods of war, all rites of birth, all knowledges pertaining to thriving in an unknown land.

We consider these old people our grandparents and remember them with love.

We say that we, their descendants, are living proof that arks work.

◎

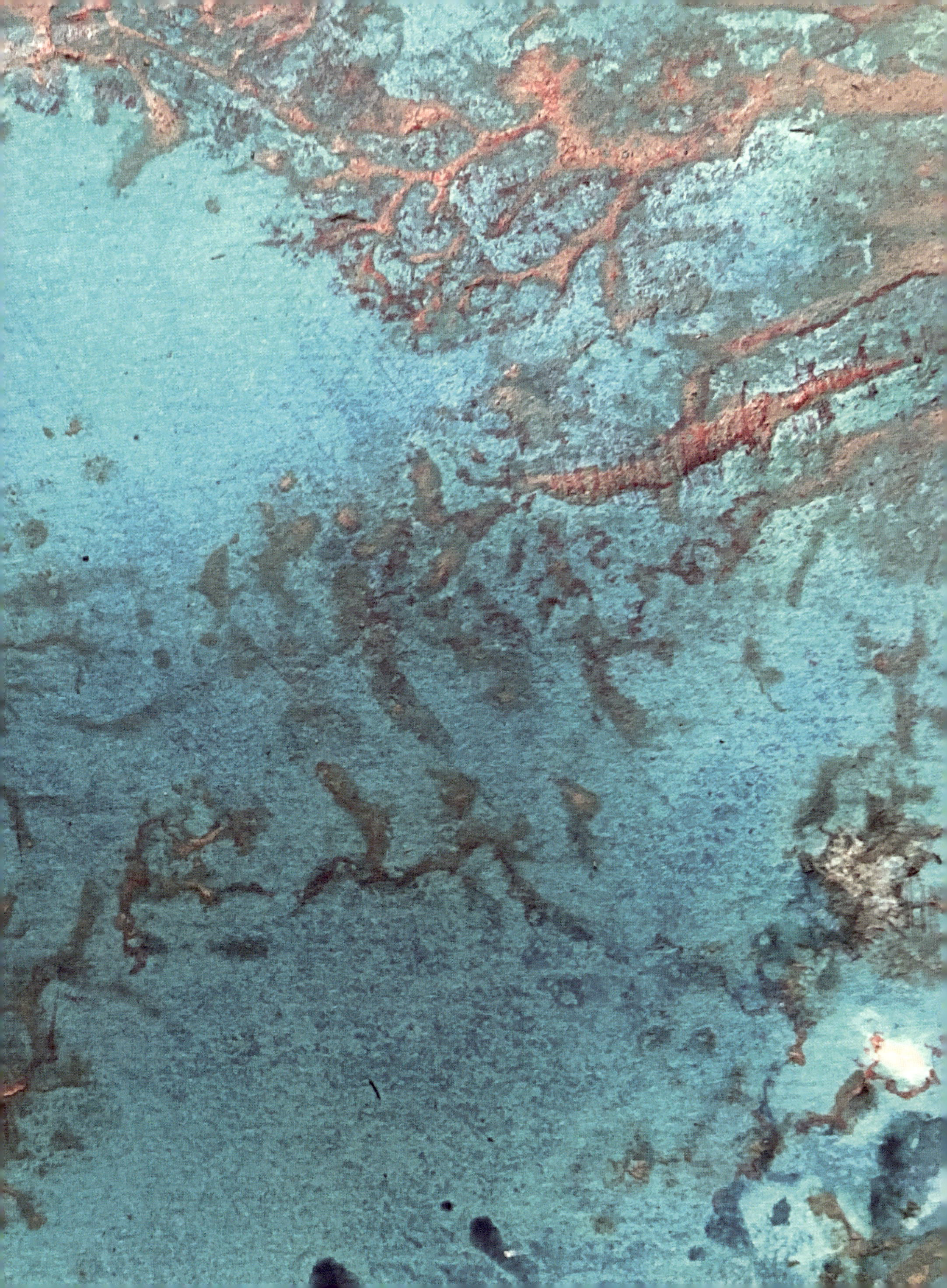

Entry DFLKJ0099E: First arrivals II, 11-- CE

A man creeps through the undergrowth beneath a canopy of towering rimu.
His kurī, ears flat, incisors bared, hangs back at his heel.

The man has heavy features, a huge jaw, sloped forehead, an animal grimace.
He and his kin are primitive savages. They do not make eye contact, or speak.

He draws back his arm, spear poised. A strange new bird, a moa, in his sights.

For the longest time, no one moves.

They remain motionless for thirty years.

Occasionally, a woman unlocks the vitrine for dusting.

It's said that this is a museum exhibit depicting racist museum exhibits.
But only when there are other Māori in the room.

◎

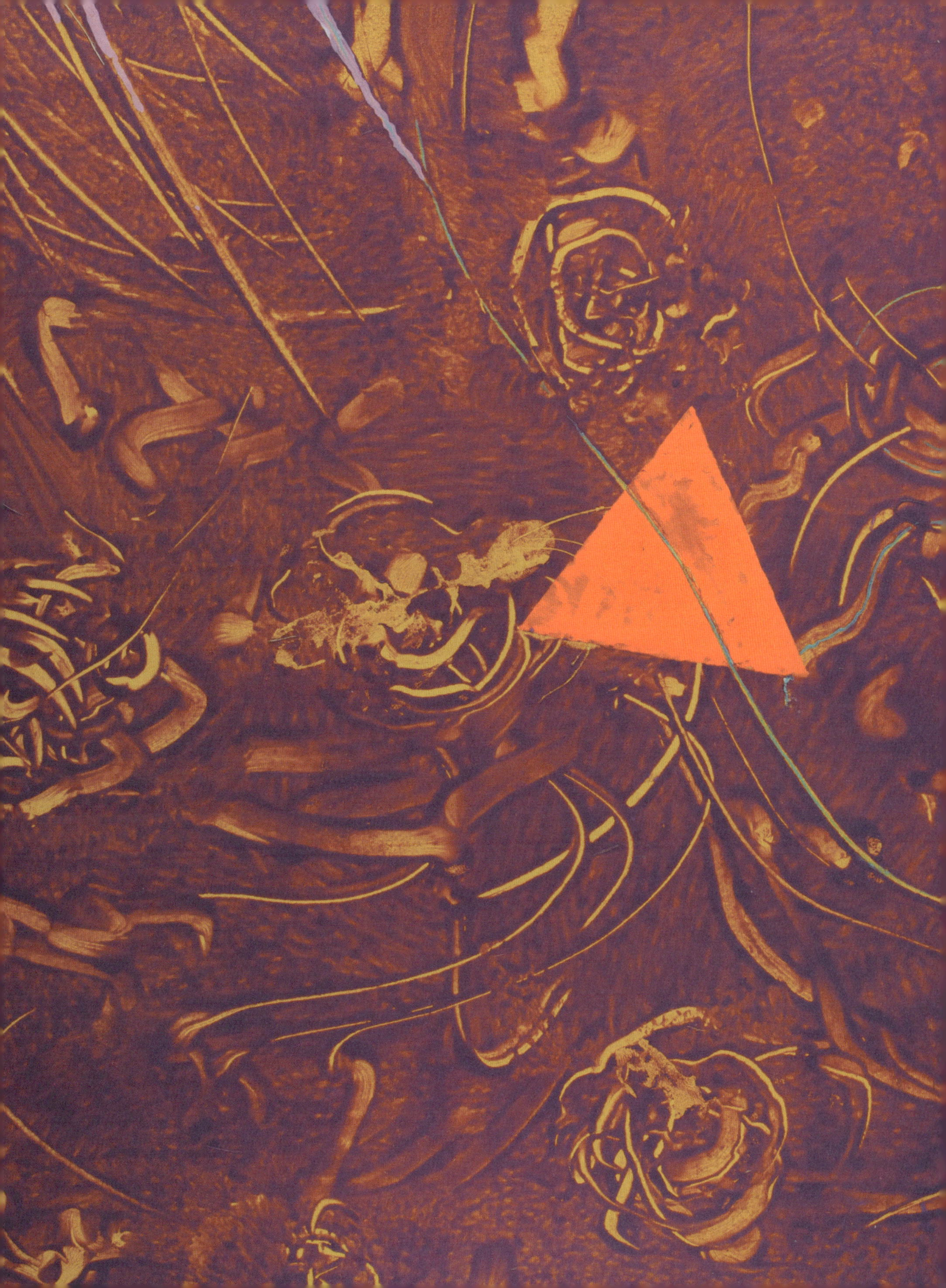

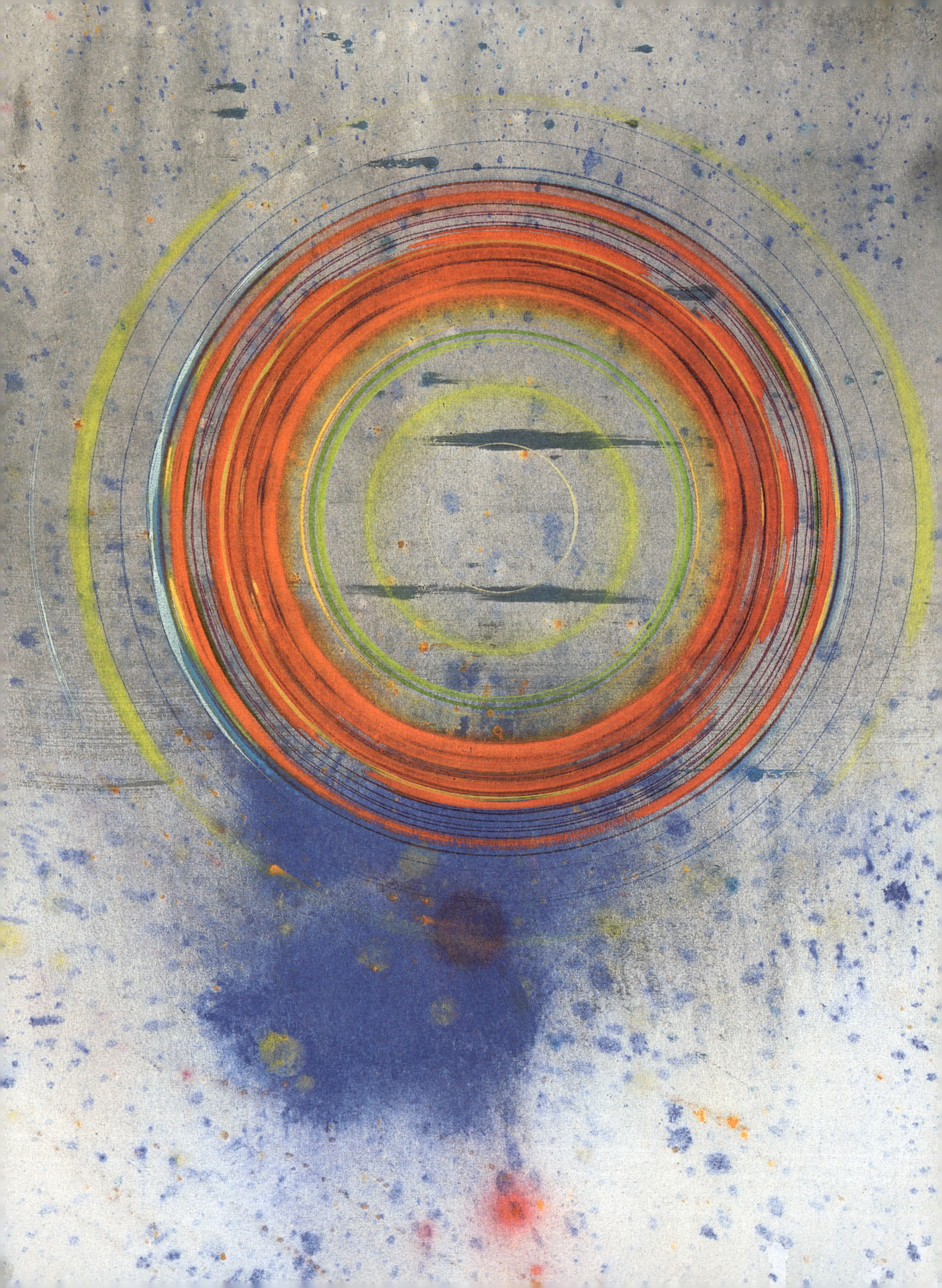

Item 33DDOX: Masonic Lodge time capsule, 1887 CE

It's been said that the time capsules gathered so far are misleading, and more representative examples are required. Here is one.

On the morning of 12 January 1887, at the intersection of Fisgard and Douglas Streets in Victoria, British Columbia, thirteen men take turns to break open the frozen ground. Their suit jackets strain across their shoulders. The capsule they bury on the site where the Masonic Temple will stand contains:

- A list of the officials involved.
- Notes to the Proceedings to organise the First Grand Communication of the Grand Lodge of British Columbia.
- Constitution of the Young Men's Christian Association.
- One heavy silver cufflink, square in profile on top, bearing the marks of small teeth.

The annihilating banality of this time capsule contains one seed of truth: what the present values may be worthless to the future.

Or, to put it differently, no one can imagine what the future will value about the past.

There were no teeth marks on the cufflink. There was no cufflink. We made that part up.

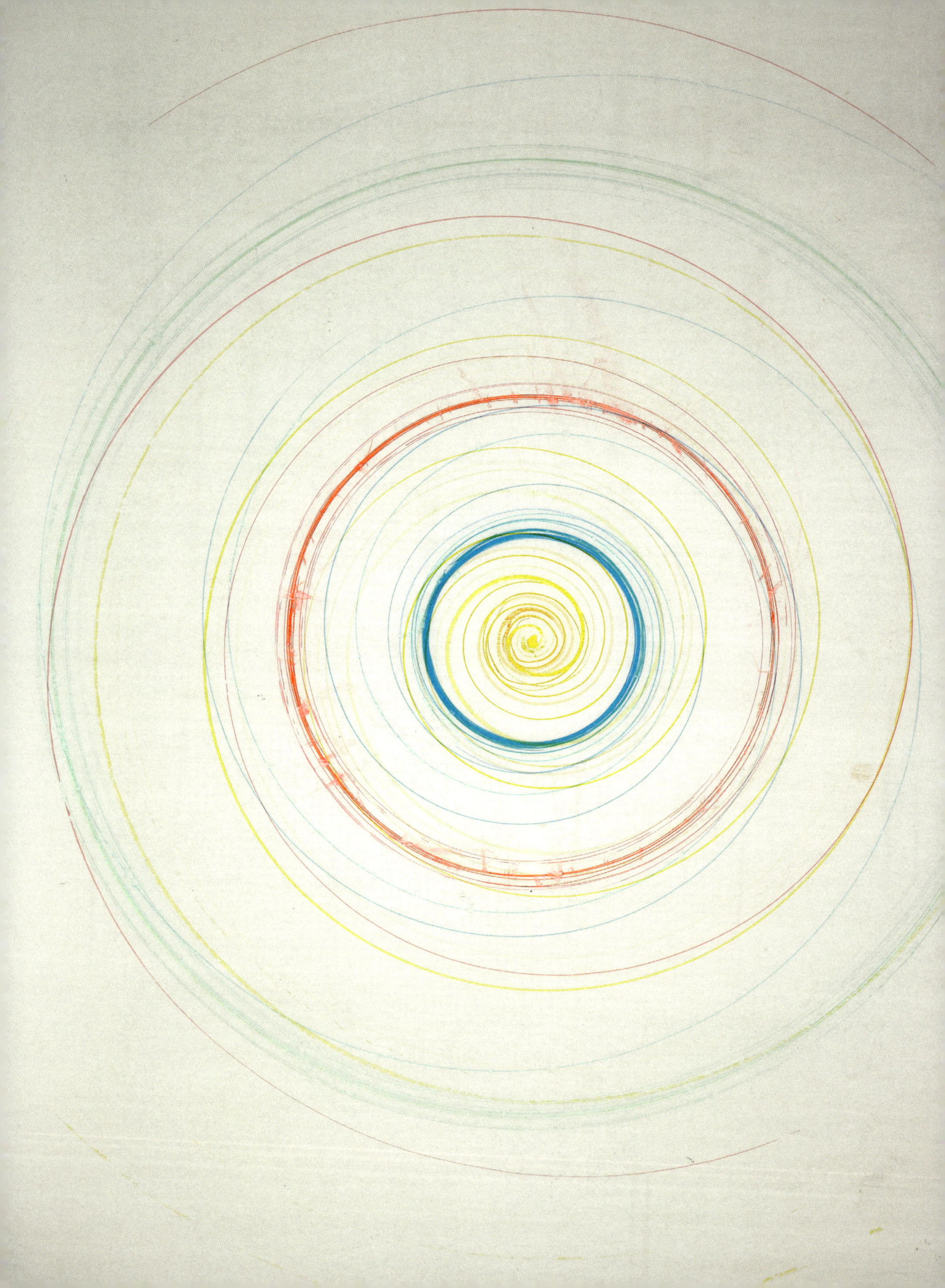

It's said that within the whare wānaka, our house of sacred learning, the realisation that we could not accurately predict what the future would value caused a crisis in our ranks. We began to argue bitterly about what the Ark of Arks should contain.

◎

TIME IS RUNNING OUT.

◎

The first explorers and colonists preserved their voyaging waka by turning them to stone.

It is said that in Murihiku, the waka *Tākitimu* was swamped by three great waves, --------, -------- and Okākā, and washed far inland, where it petrified into the mountain range bearing its name.

It is said that the greatest of our earthly ancestors, Aoraki, brought his waka down from the heavens alongside his brothers, intent on meeting their father's new wife, Papatūānuku, the Earth mother.

It's said that in those days there was nothing but ocean. After months of sailing, the brothers found nothing: a watery world that could have been from before or after the flood.

They chose to return home, but a hapa in Aoraki's karakia saw the waka wrecked on an undersea reef. The brothers sat awaiting rescue atop the overturned hull for so long their hair turned white, their bodies to stone.

That waka is our island. Those mountains are our ancestors. We descend from that stone.

Though I have never heard it said, I suspect this kōrero immortalises the moment when our ancestors realised they could no longer return to Hawaiki.

Every hapū makes a time capsule of their land.

◎

TIME IS RUNNING

◎

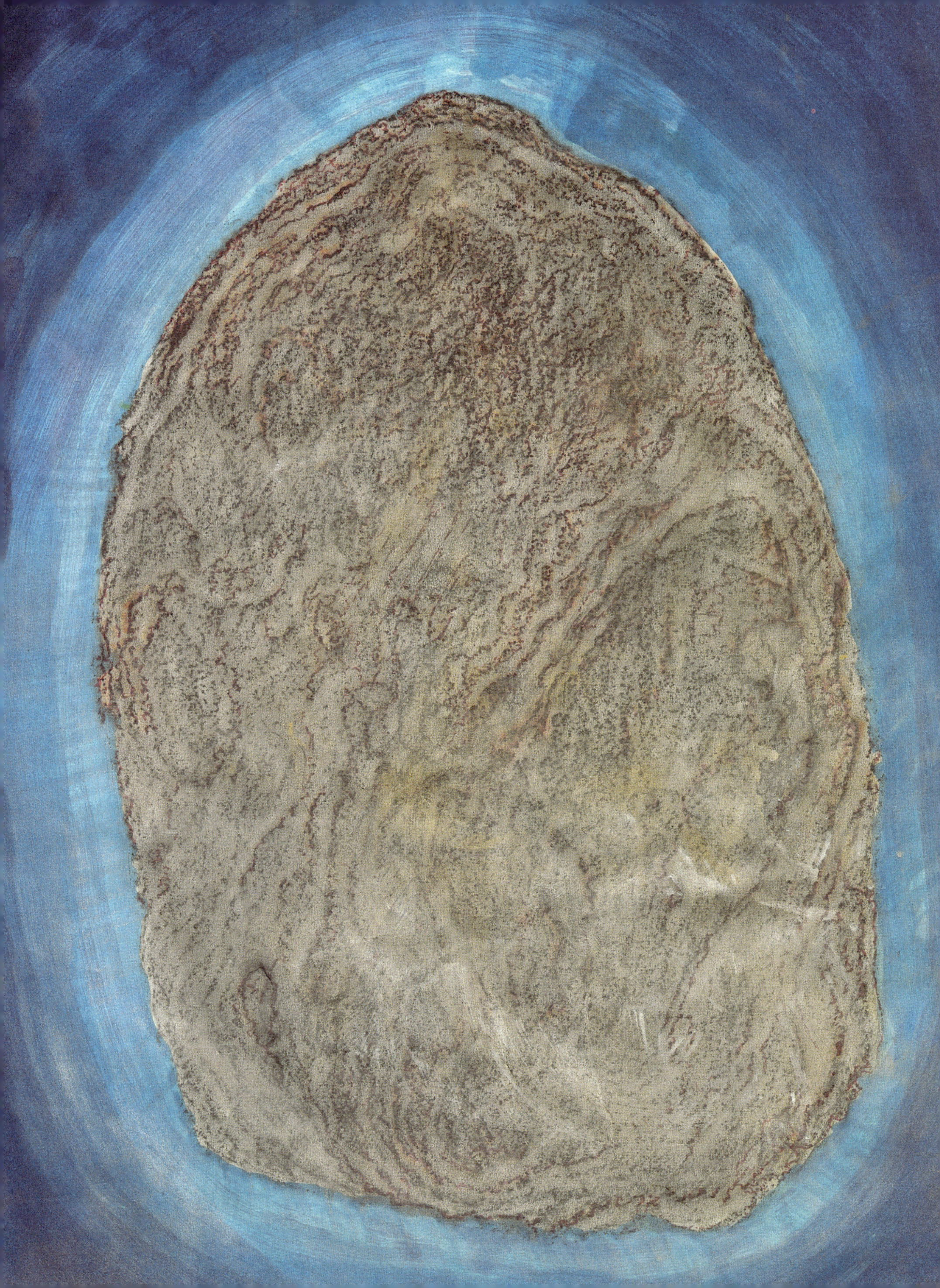

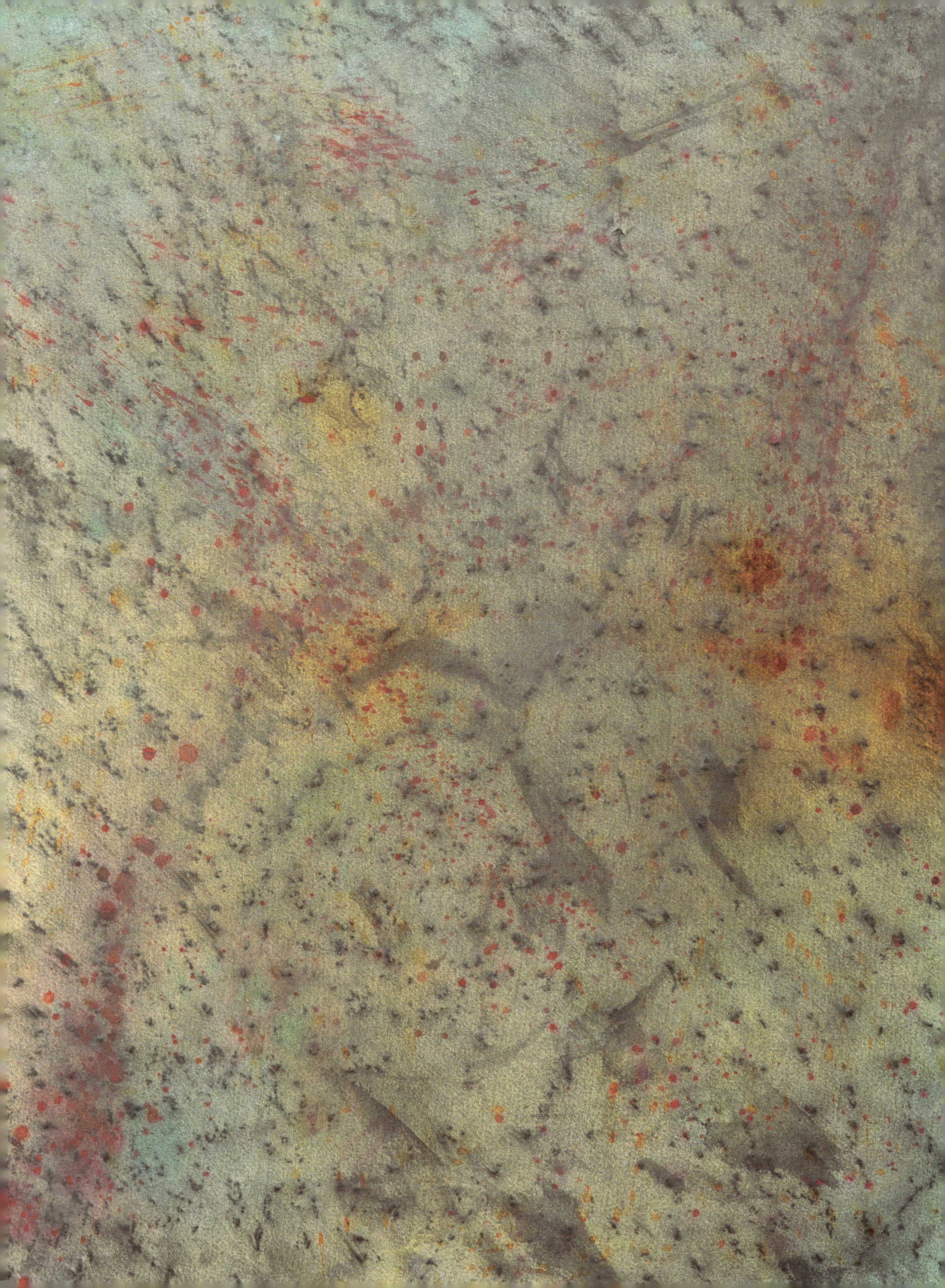

It is said that Noah decided to leave nothing behind.

It is said that seven scribes sat at the entrance to his ark and listed every living thing that went aboard. They wrote their inventory on a sequence of clay tablets.

Given the 8.7 million species of animal and plant recorded, the dimensions of each tablet and the dimensions of the ark, our leading biblical scholars, Tūtetaumata and Māhere, made this startling discovery: the volume of the complete set of tablets is a perfect match for the volume of the ark.

They concluded that there were no animals or plants aboard.

Rather, the ark contained a list of the plants and animals in existence at that time.

Noah's Library would be a more fitting name.

◎

TIME IS

◎

I have been working on our Ark of Arks for a long time.

Before the wider project started in earnest, I was already cataloguing the things previous civilisations sought to insulate from time: religious treasures, vanity projects, blueprints, pūrākau, spiritual principles, waiata, ephemera, dust.

It is said, by my friends, that this is an infinite and futile task.

It is said that when a person undertakes an infinite and futile task there is something more important they are putting off.

I am putting off writing down the things I want my son to know about me, and our world, before I, and they, are gone.

◎

--------, --------.

◎

TIME

◎

It's said that in the old days, all our arks were people but only some of our people were arks.

◎

It's said that once our whare wānaka broke into factions, things unravelled, but in useful ways.

It's said that those of us who had disowned representation and started collecting real objects immediately began to fill the wharenui at Ōraka.

It's said that four months into our collection of objects, the wharenui was full and no person could enter.

We built a pātaka, a giant, raised tilt-slab storehouse, with carved serpentine figures adorning the external blast-proof walls, and filled this too.

It is said we gave our speeches outside in the rain.

◎

TIME IS

◎

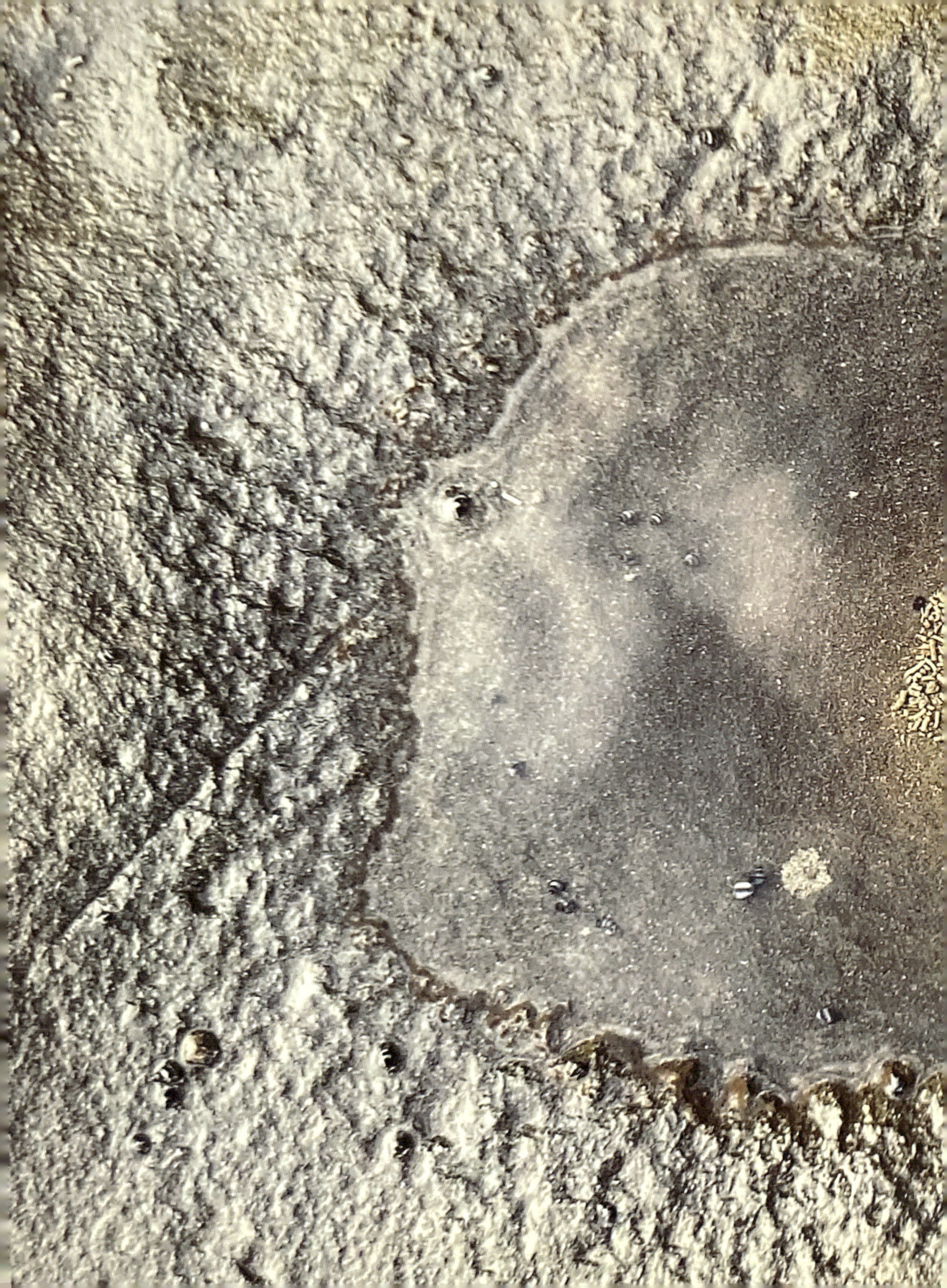

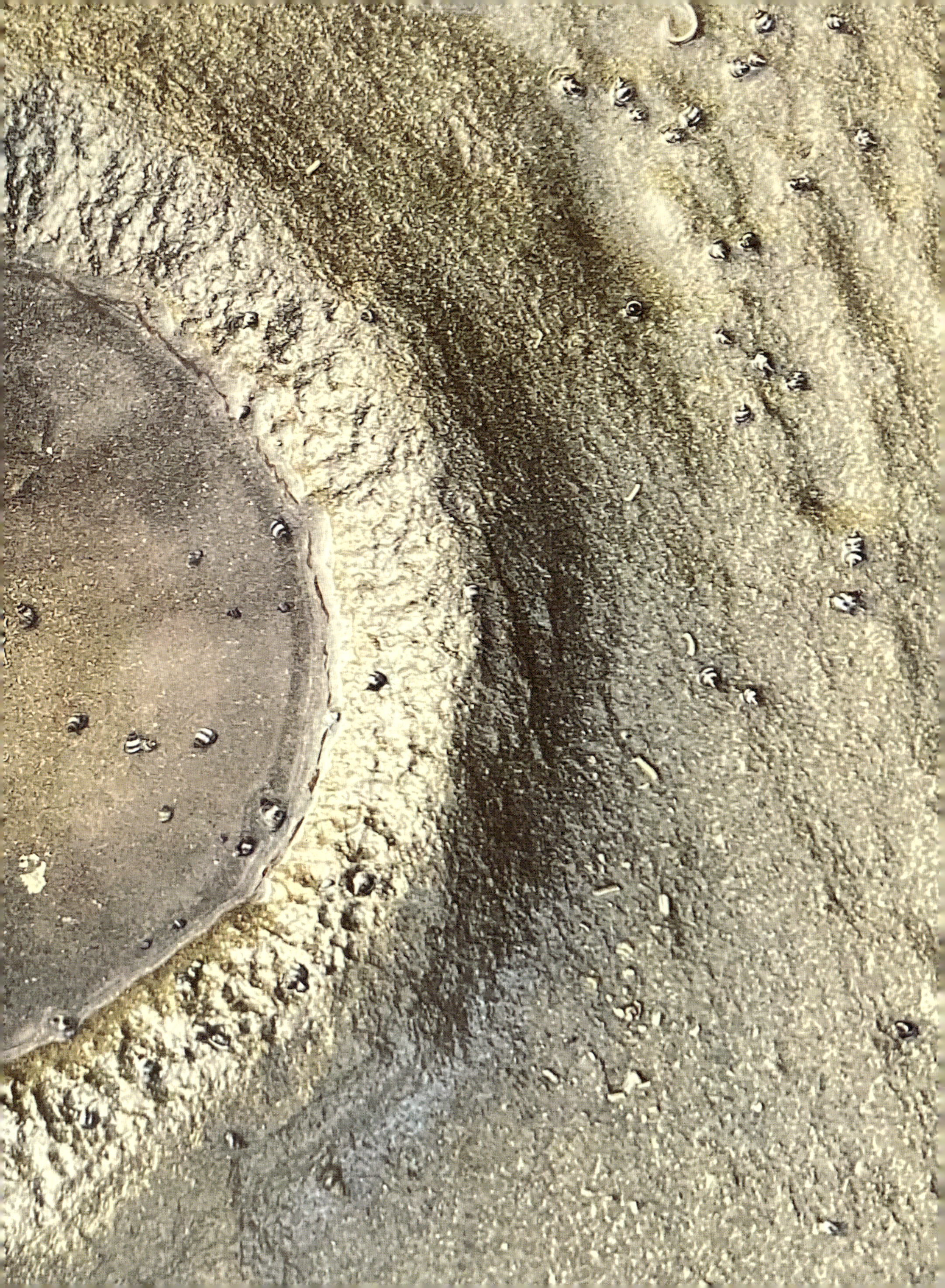

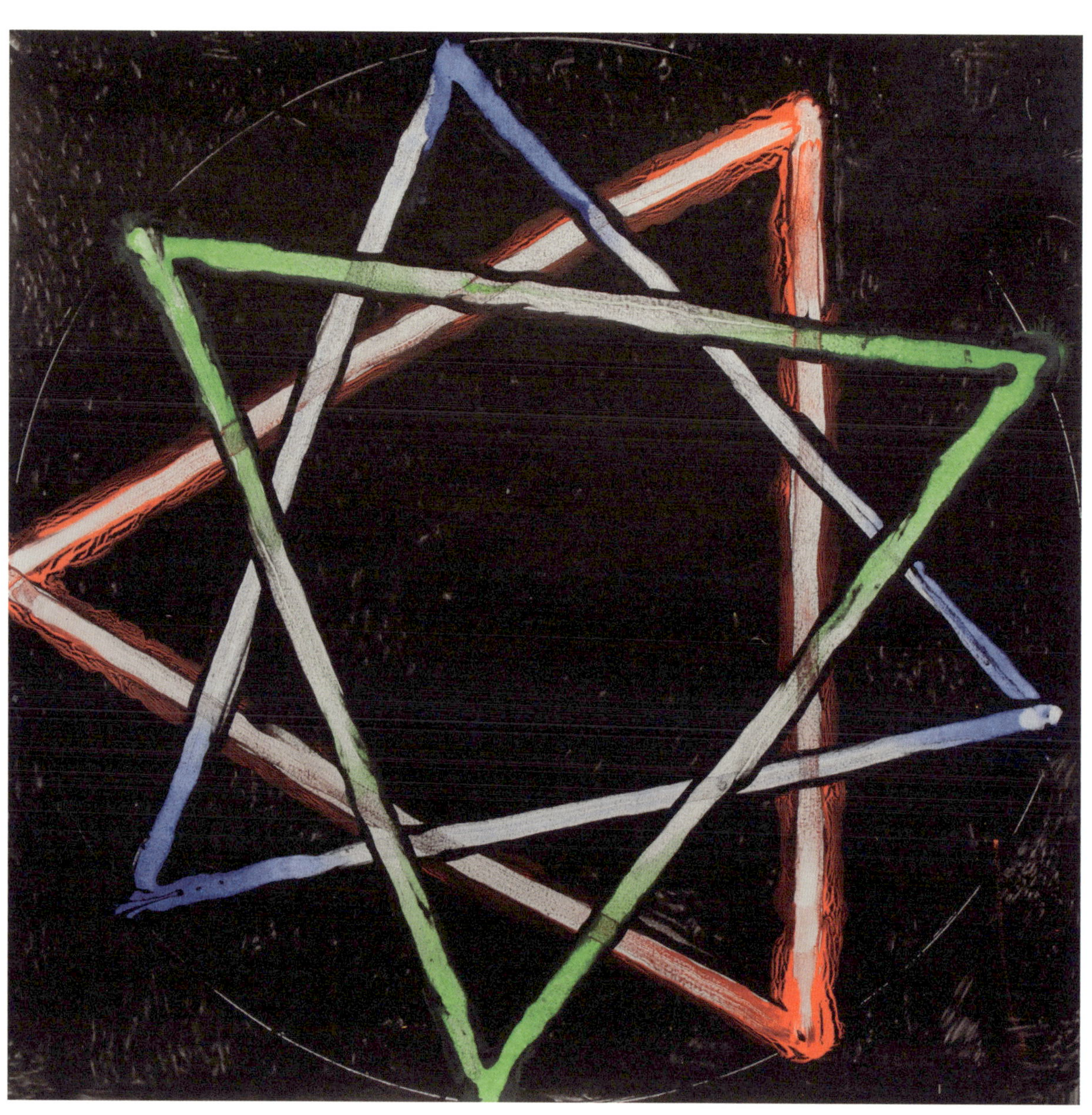

Item SDOIFU-0340: Seeds of language I, 200 BCE

It is said that 200 years before the birth of Christ, after a period of catastrophic flooding of the Nile, the Greek king Ptolemy distributed gifts of corn to his Egyptian subjects.

It's said the old Egyptian temples posted decrees, carved in stone, announcing and honouring these gifts.

It's said that the Romans closed the old Egyptian temples, and that later occupying civilisations used such temples as quarries.

In the 1400s, the great patron of art and architecture Sultan Qaitbay built a fort at Rashid, on the west bank of the Nile, with stone mined from ruined temples which had themselves been built with stone hewn from still older temples.

It's said that in 1799 Napoleon's expeditionary forces occupied Qaitbay's fort. As Ottoman troops prepared to attack, the French scrambled to strengthen the defences.

Teams of soldiers, stripped to their breeches, set to work mining an old wall for its stone. Amid the dust and clatter they noticed one curious stone inscribed with three distinct scripts.

Lieutenant Pierre-François Bouchard was curious. Could this be the same message in three different languages?

It was: a decree, written in Egyptian demotic script, hieroglyphics and Greek, about King Ptolemy's gifts of corn. 'La Pierre de Rosette', the French called it.

This ark carried two secrets: the secret of hieroglyphics and the secret of how much is preserved through random chance.

It's said that disillusionment grew within the ranks of the whare wānaka as our research identified many more such unintentional time capsules and arks.

It's said that a further faction formed, of those convinced that our efforts were wasted. They came to believe that the true and perfect medium of preservation was randomness.

It's said that their leader, Tūtetaumata, spent a winter's night going through the wharenui selecting our greatest treasures. His friends surprised him on the beach at dawn, knee-deep in the surf, which was by now metres from the whare's door. He was throwing our treasures into the sea. A light snow fell.

◎

TIME IS RUNNING

◎

I want to record what was passed on to me.

I received a heavy woven poncho that warmed my father through the 1970s.

I received my mother's confidence and my father's gentleness, though each may falter.

I received the knowledge that I belong to this land.

I received strong lungs and weak eyes.

I received clean rivers.

I received the gift of curiosity, and the generalist's curse.

I was given --------, but not --------.

Ahi, my ark, four years old, now dancing, now making jokes, now asking me to be a baby having a bad dream so you can comfort my cries: what of value can I pass on to you?

I will bequeath you my phone, and my laptop, my hard drives, my eReader, my tablet, my smart watch.

None of my grandparents could have dreamed of these treasures.

All of these treasures will be obsolete.

There are no heirlooms in the age of tech.

It is said that we found ways to pass on clean rivers, but so far this is a lie.

◎

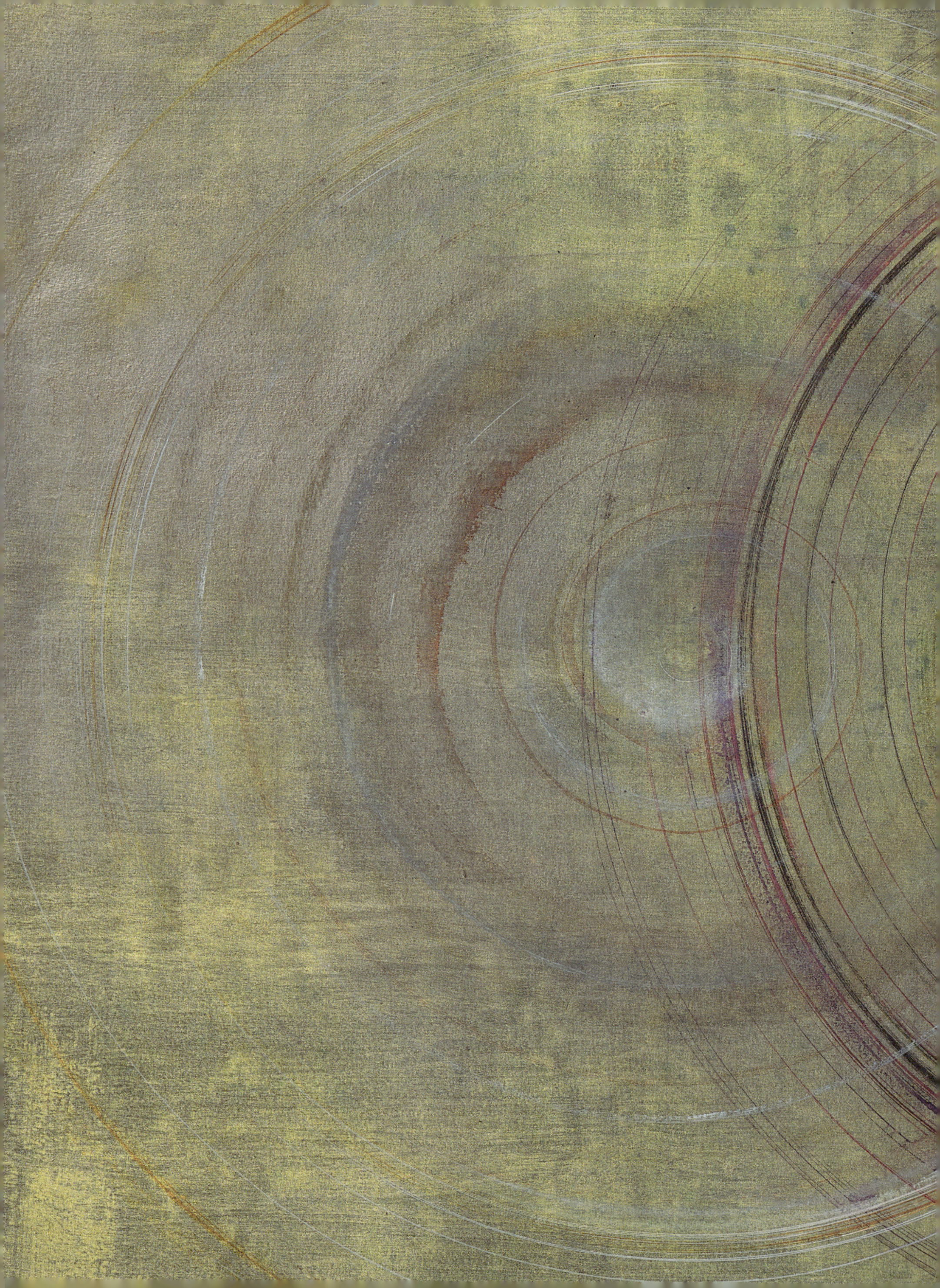

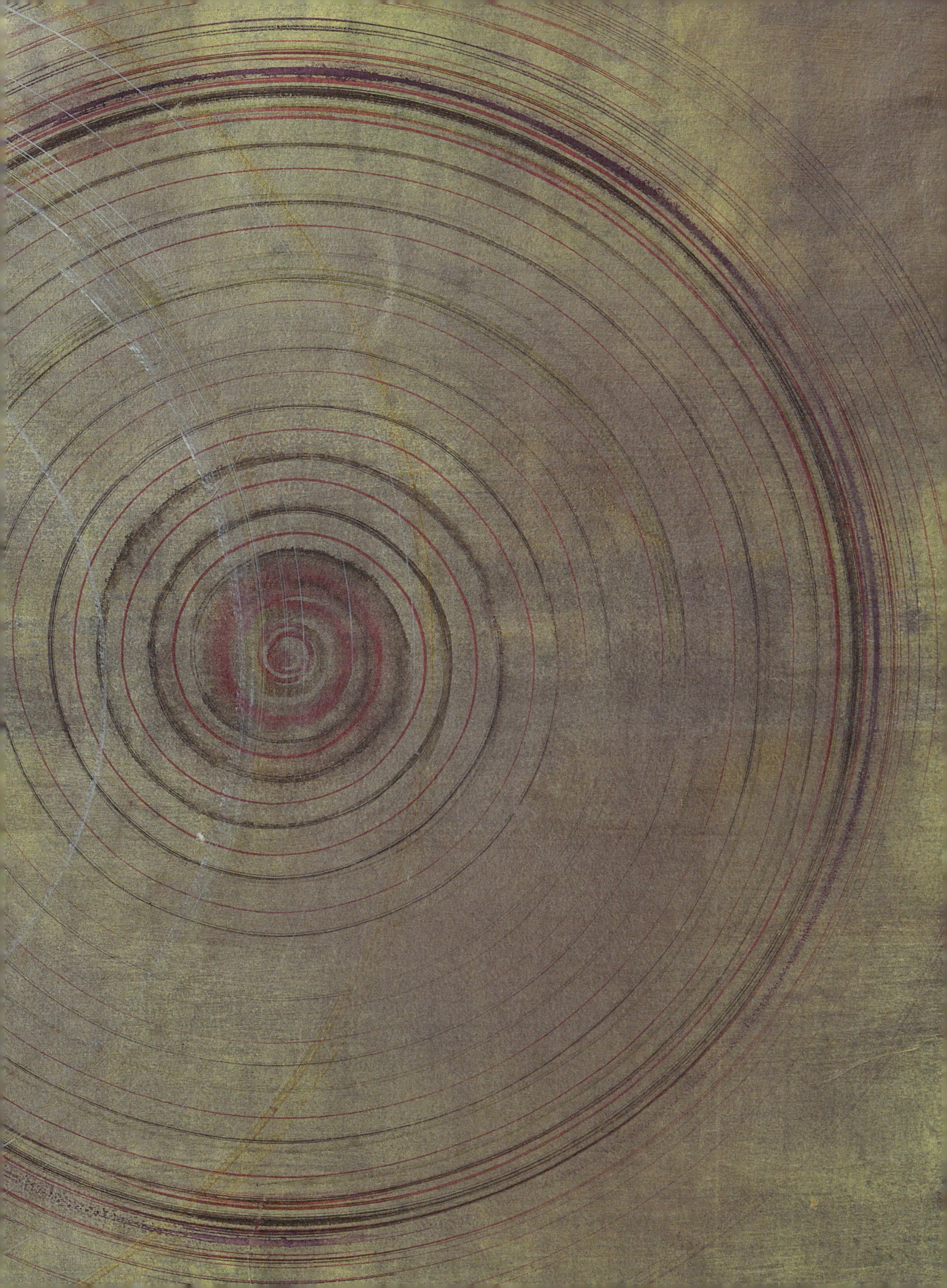

It's said Noah beached on a mountaintop. But it's the mountaintop we want.

We had our best engineers draw up plans to preserve Aoraki and his snow and his ice. Without them, our ancestor will collapse into ruin.

Our best engineers concluded the only material capable of preserving Aoraki is time, which we have already spent.

◎

Most time capsules are forgotten the instant the last shovelful of earth is tamped down.

◎

TIME IS RUNNING OUT

◎

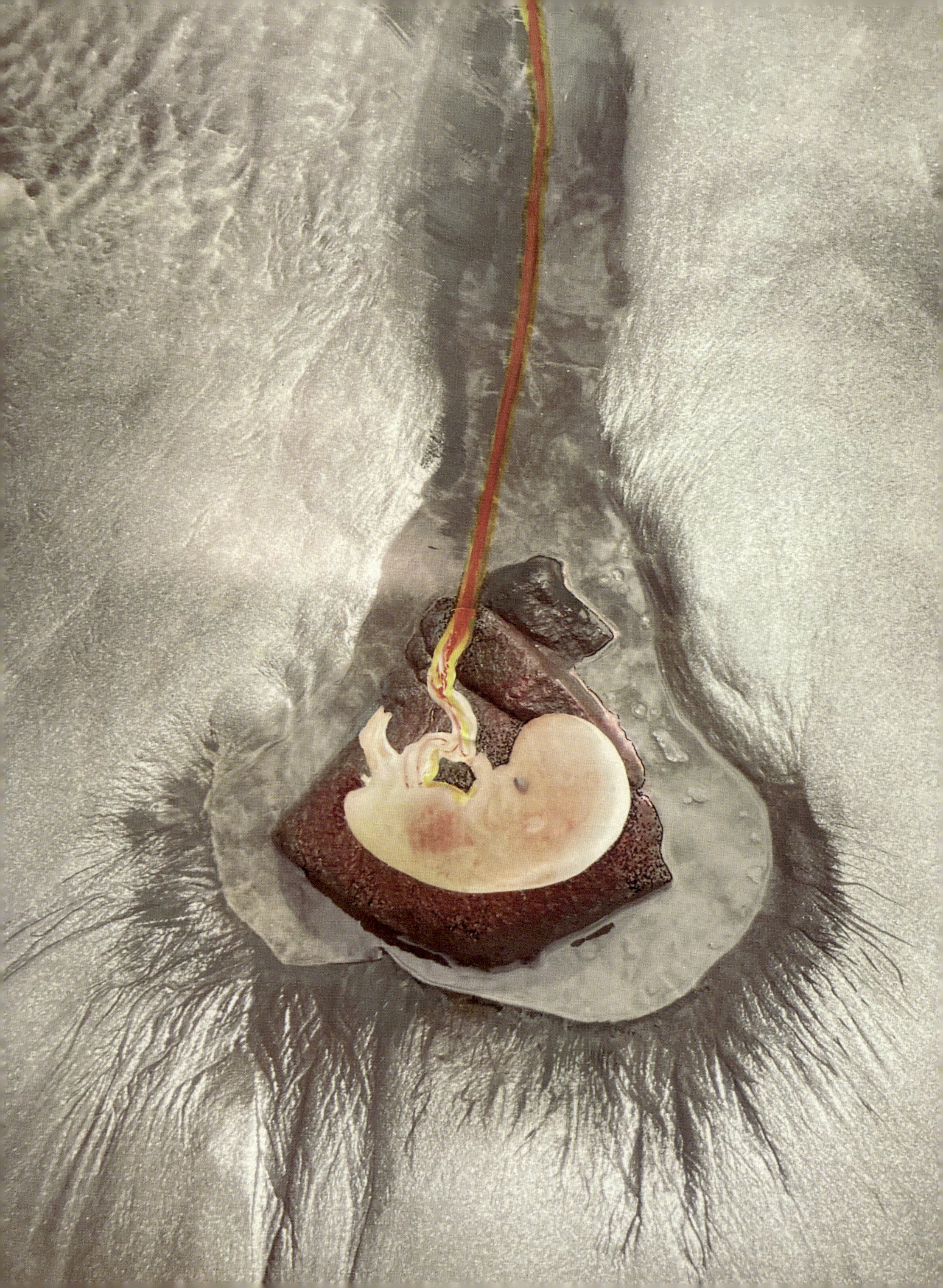

Item SFDOUS098403: KEO satellite, 1994 CE

It is said that the KEO satellite was designed to be shot into space on an orbit that will return it to earth in 50,000 years.

Fifty thousand years ago, humans began drawing on the walls of caves.

It is said the KEO satellite contains a synthetic diamond that encloses samples of earth, water and air, and a drop of blood. The human genome is engraved on one face.

It is said the satellite's data contains an encyclopaedic 'Contemporary Library of Alexandria': the knowledge, habits and customs of '21st-century man'.

It is said that there is sufficient data storage on board for every living person on Earth to record a message to their future descendants.

What would you tell your great-grandchildren about your life, your expectations, your doubts, your desires, your values, your emotions, your dreams?

Collection of such messages has been ongoing for more than a decade. If you lack the internet, post your message to: KEO, BP 100, 75262 PARIS Cedex 06, France.

It is said the KEO satellite is the size of a large beach ball, made of titanium and engraved with the Earth's image.

Upon re-entering Earth's atmosphere in the year 52,023, the outer layer will combust. A blazing artificial aurora will announce its arrival home.

The data aboard KEO is stored on glass DVDs.

To overcome the possibility that our far-future mokopuna will lack DVD players, it's said that the project's engineers included pictograms detailing how to build a DVD player from scratch.

It is thought that in the future, given the march of progress, fashioning the alloys, lasers, electricity and motors required to build a DVD player using only a set of IKEA-style instructions should be relatively straightforward.

The launch of KEO was delayed in 1996, 2001, 2003, 2006, 2008, 2011, 2012, 2013 and 2016. As of 2023, the proposed launch date is 2019.

The project's creator, conceptual artist Jean-Marc Philippe, died in 2008.

We of the whare wānaka delighted in the idea of a time capsule that was forgotten before it even existed.

◎

Entry 344XKSS-1: Seeds of language II

(Crying in shock): Tīhei mauriora! Purpled, face screwed against the world's sudden light.

'Da.' A syllable untethered to the world.

'Dat!' Pointing emphatically. Something separated from everything. *Dat.*

'Anō!' More. Again. More kai, more games, lift me cuddle me close, again. Said with joy. Words as cause of effect.

'Ai-dah-dah.' You-do-this-now. Point at the sandpit, point at me, point at the truck: 'Ai-dah-dah.' Language as lever to move the world.

I would preserve these words for our whānau.

I would not preserve them in a metal sphere and fire them into outer space.

Would I put them in a book?

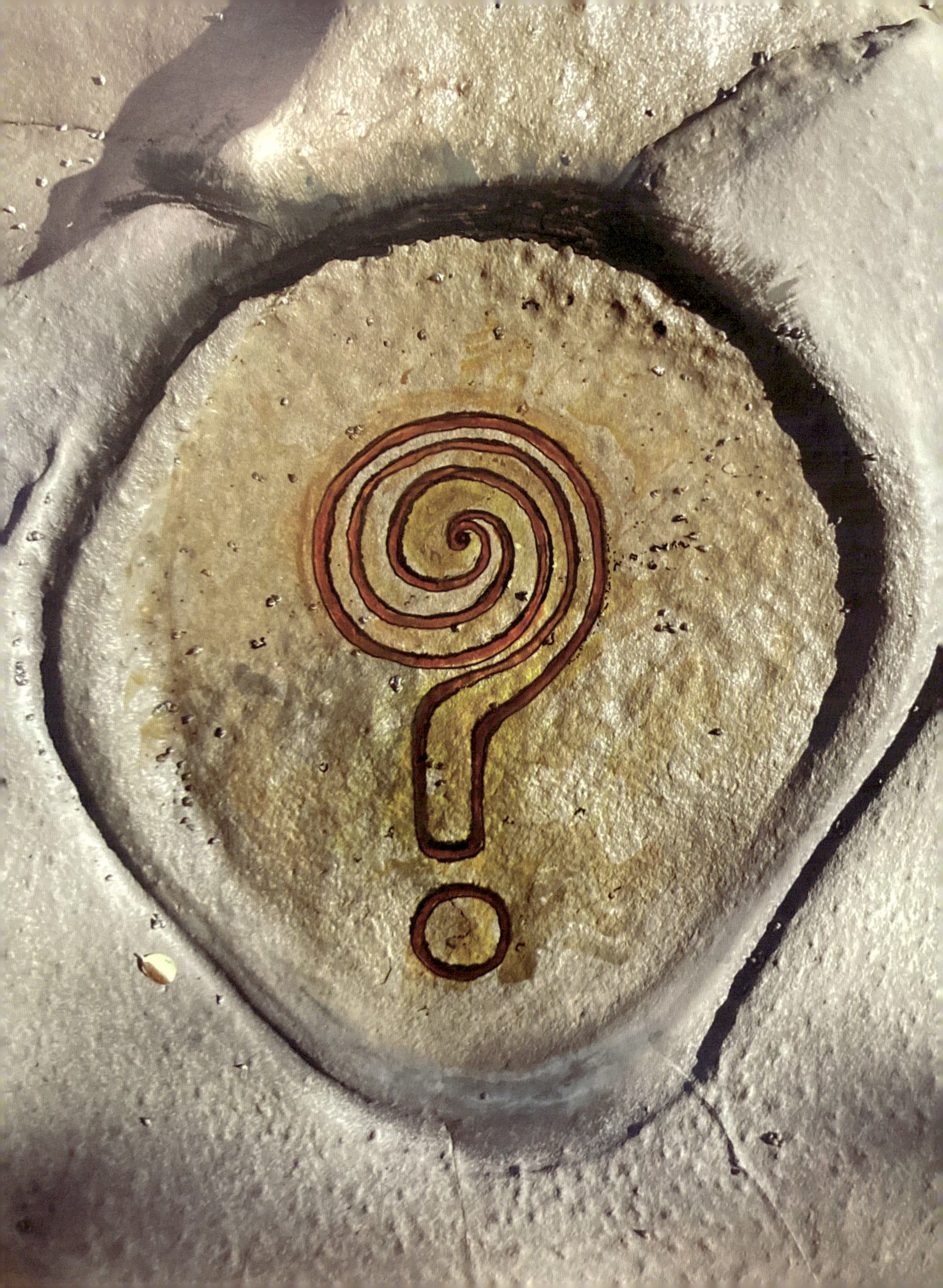

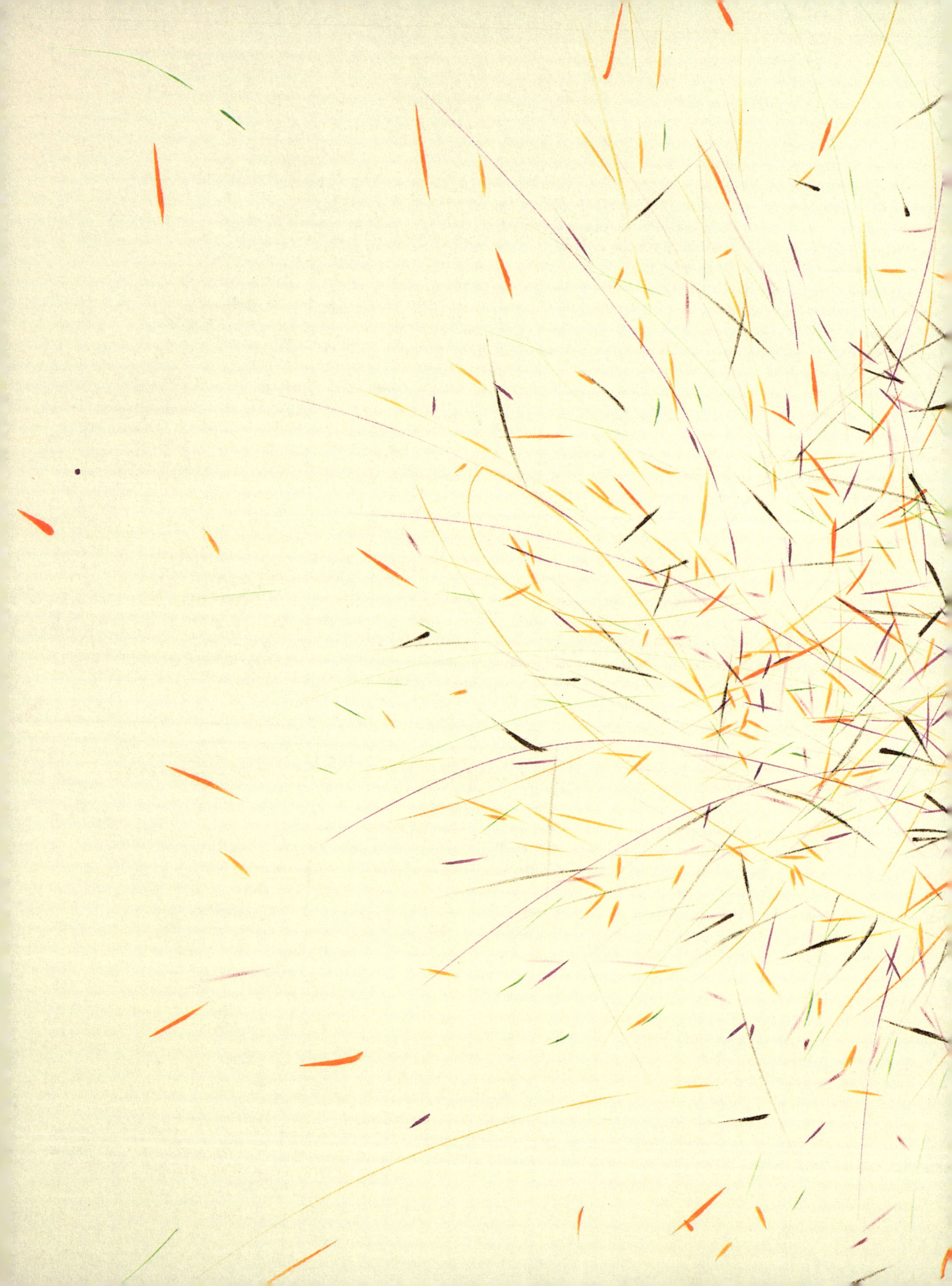

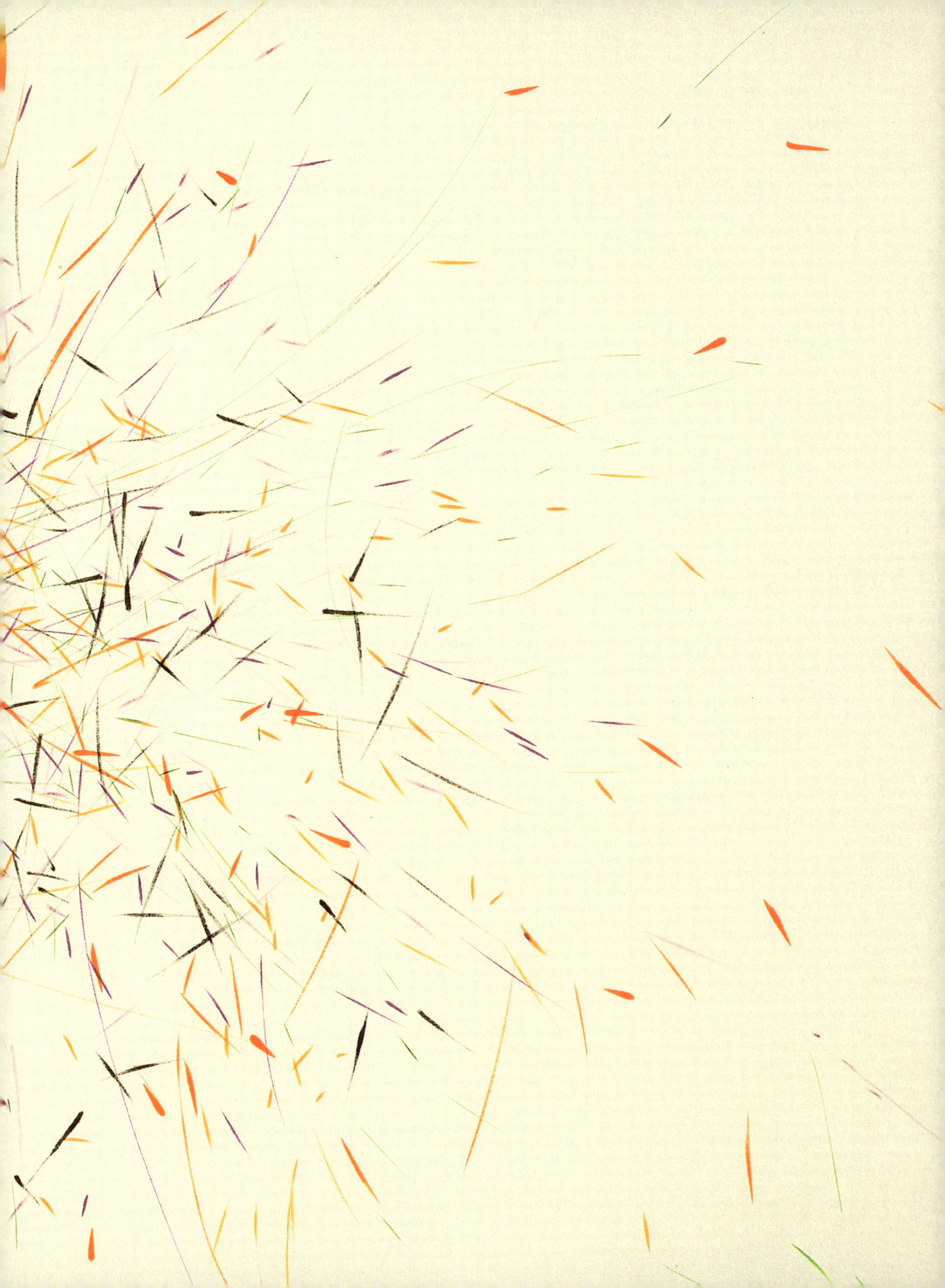

Item DLKJ__32W9

Stones Taro Papa Nugs Levitation Foodman Remix Mount Kimbie Q Zap Francis Human Mover.

It's said that we preserved all of Spotify's playlists but none of the songs.

◎

TIME IS RUNNING OUT OF

◎

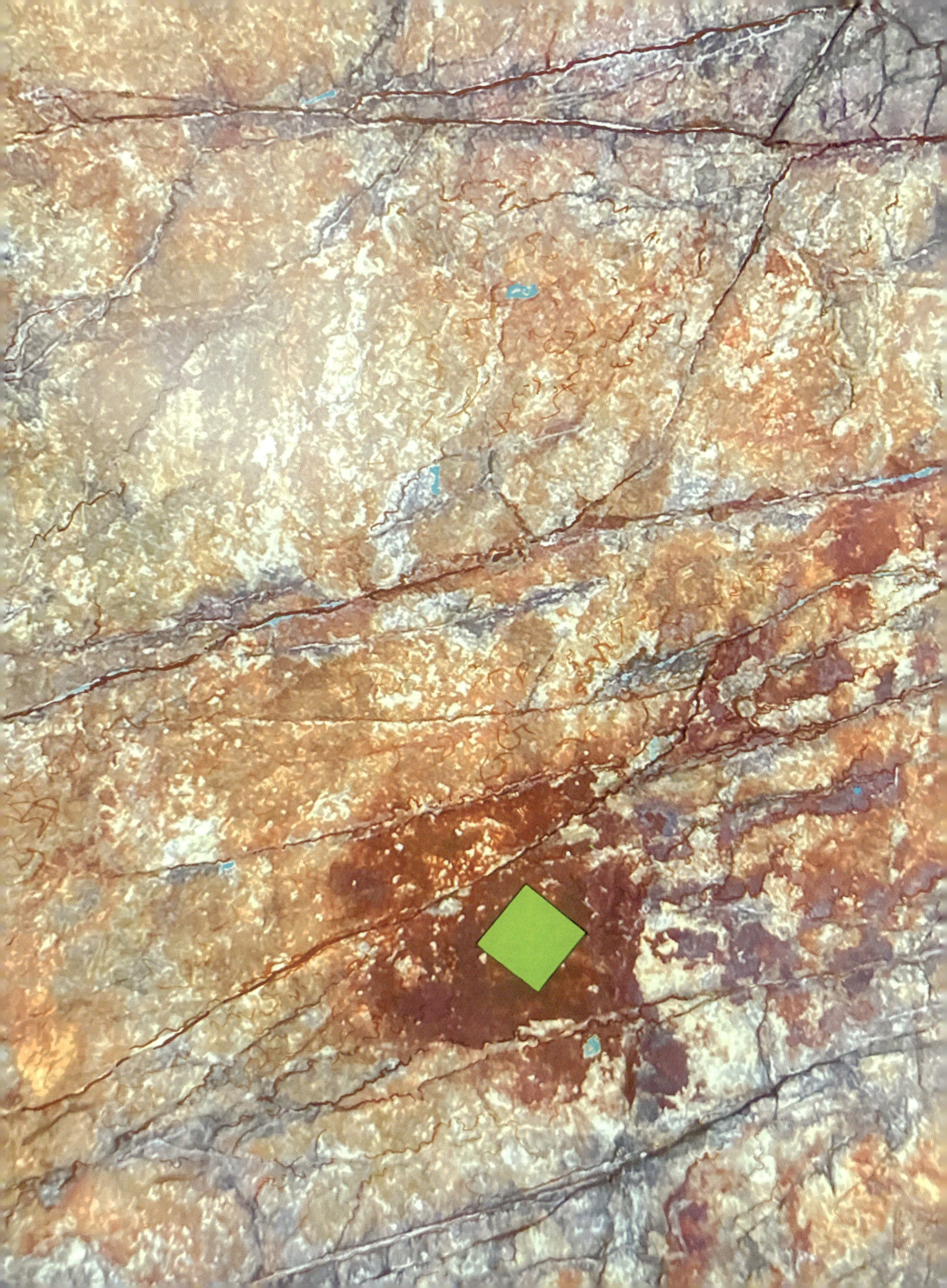

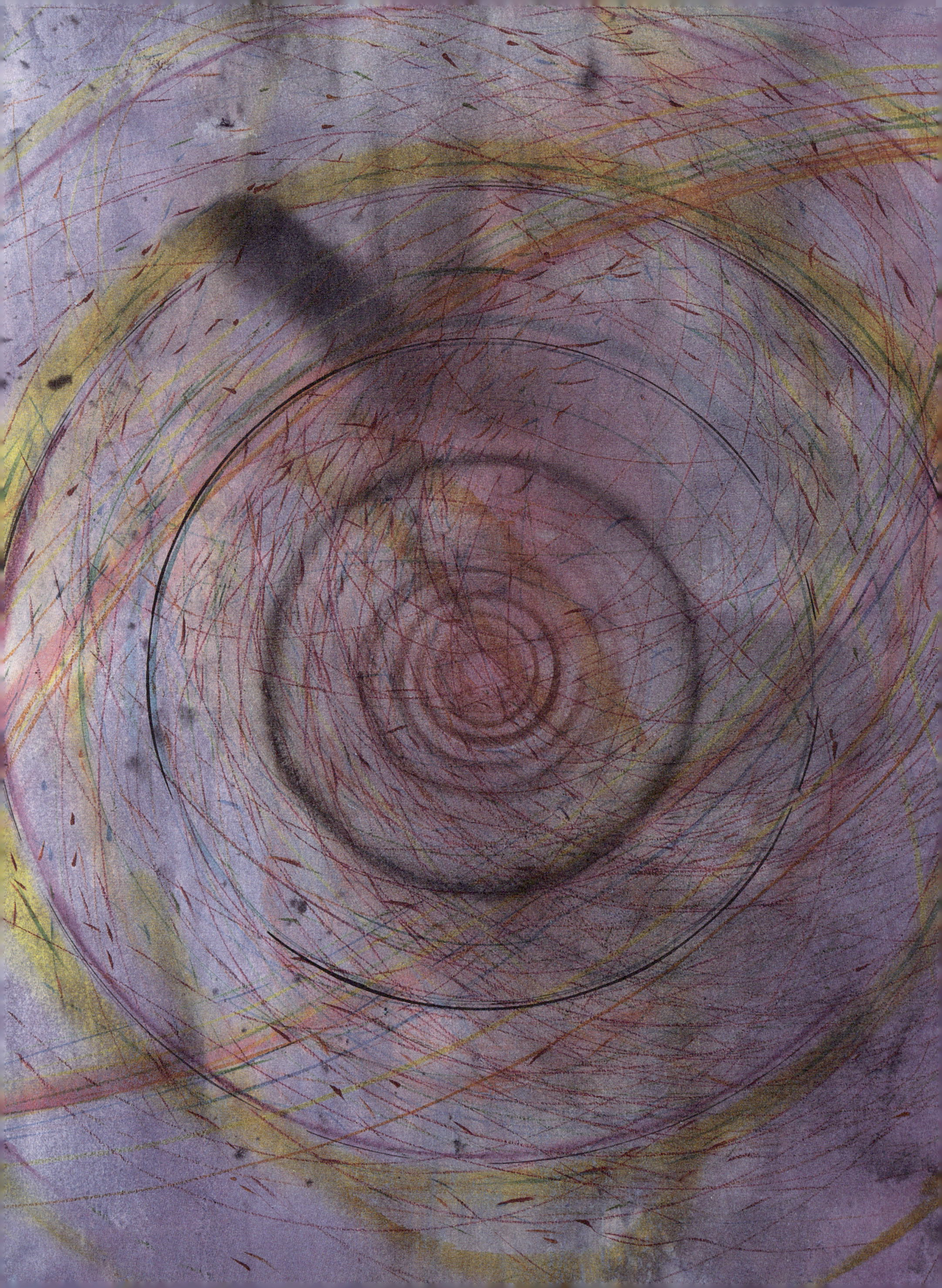

Item 23098KLKJJJVV: Memory of Mankind

It's said that cave paintings are our earliest attempt to preserve information in physical form.

It's said that we are storing nearly 100 zettabytes of data today.

It's said that if you spuriously assume that search-engine queries represent genuine desire, in 2022 humans were most interested in information about: Wordle, India vs England, Ukraine, Queen Elizabeth, Ind vs SA, World Cup, India v West Indies, iPhone 14.

One hundred zettabytes cannot be visualised using the traditional metric of X football fields.

One hundred zettabytes can be visualised as 305,000 cricket grounds packed with people each videoing themselves for 6000 years.

It's said the act of recording is now more important than what is being recorded.

In hyperscale data centres, the servers have no blinking lights. There is nothing but warm darkness and the *om* of a quarter of a million spinning fans.

It's said that our data habits trend towards the impossible: in 150 years we will need to store more bytes of data than there are atoms on Earth.

We conceive of the internet as ephemeral: the cloud and the web. This is correct. Digital texts are more fragile than books, or rocks.

Servers are threatened by power cuts, water, fire, magnetic radiation, shock, bankruptcy, sand, dust, corrosion and coronal mass ejection.

Ceramic tablets are threatened by hammers.

The Memory of Mankind (MoM) project, housed in an Austrian salt mine, aims to preserve human knowledge by transcribing the internet onto ceramic tablets.

Content for MoM comes from universities, the general public, and Facebook profiles drawn randomly from the web.

It's thought that future civilisations will be ambivalent about finding Facebook profiles drawn randomly from the web.

It's said the project's choice of ceramics was inspired by Sumerian clay tablets.

It's rarely said that the project's choice of name was inspired by sexism.

The archive includes the location of nuclear waste dumps.

Those who contribute to the MoM project receive a ceramic disk showing the location of the salt mine. They are asked to pass this on to their children.

The archive is self-sealing: 200 years of natural salt accretion will automatically close the access shafts.

It's said that the archive is designed to remain hidden from 'immature civilisations'. Deciphering the token's map and locating the tablets deep underground will require equivalent technology to our own.

It's said that if a future civilisation develops satellite maps and ground-penetrating radar, it will already have generated its own archival material identical to that contained within MoM.

It's said that if you believe in destiny, such a civilisation will share ours.

◎

Item DSKJ323022: Carved alabaster disk, 2300 BCE

It's said that a carved alabaster disk, shaped like the full moon, unearthed from the rubble of ancient Ur, contains the name of the first named author: Enheduanna, priestess of the moon god Nanna.

It's said that around 2300 BCE Enheduanna penned the Sumerian Temple Hymns.

Her hymns were sung to the temples, acknowledging those whare as living beings, as we do.

O Kesh like holy Aratta
inside is a womb dark and deep
your outside towers over
all

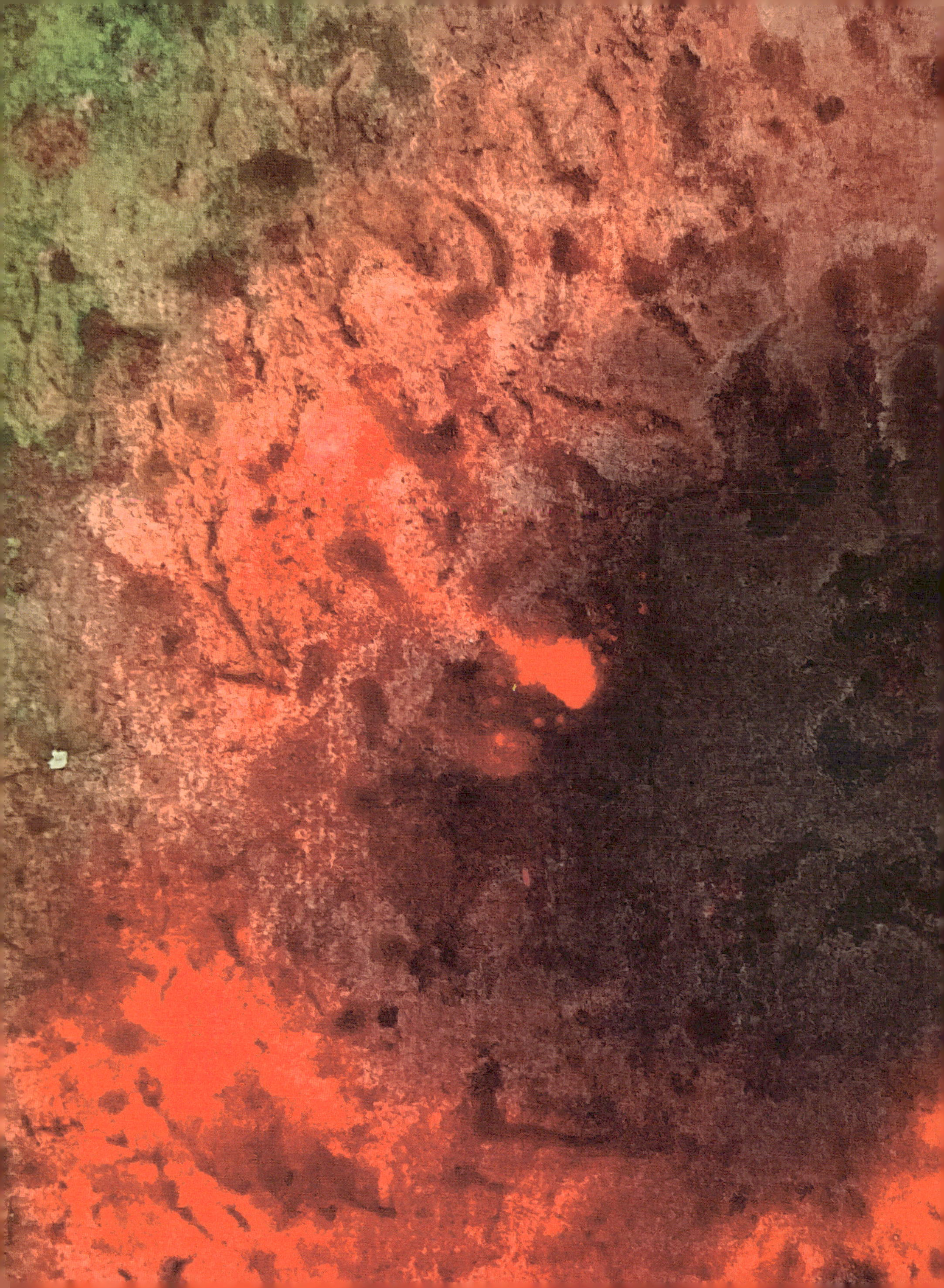

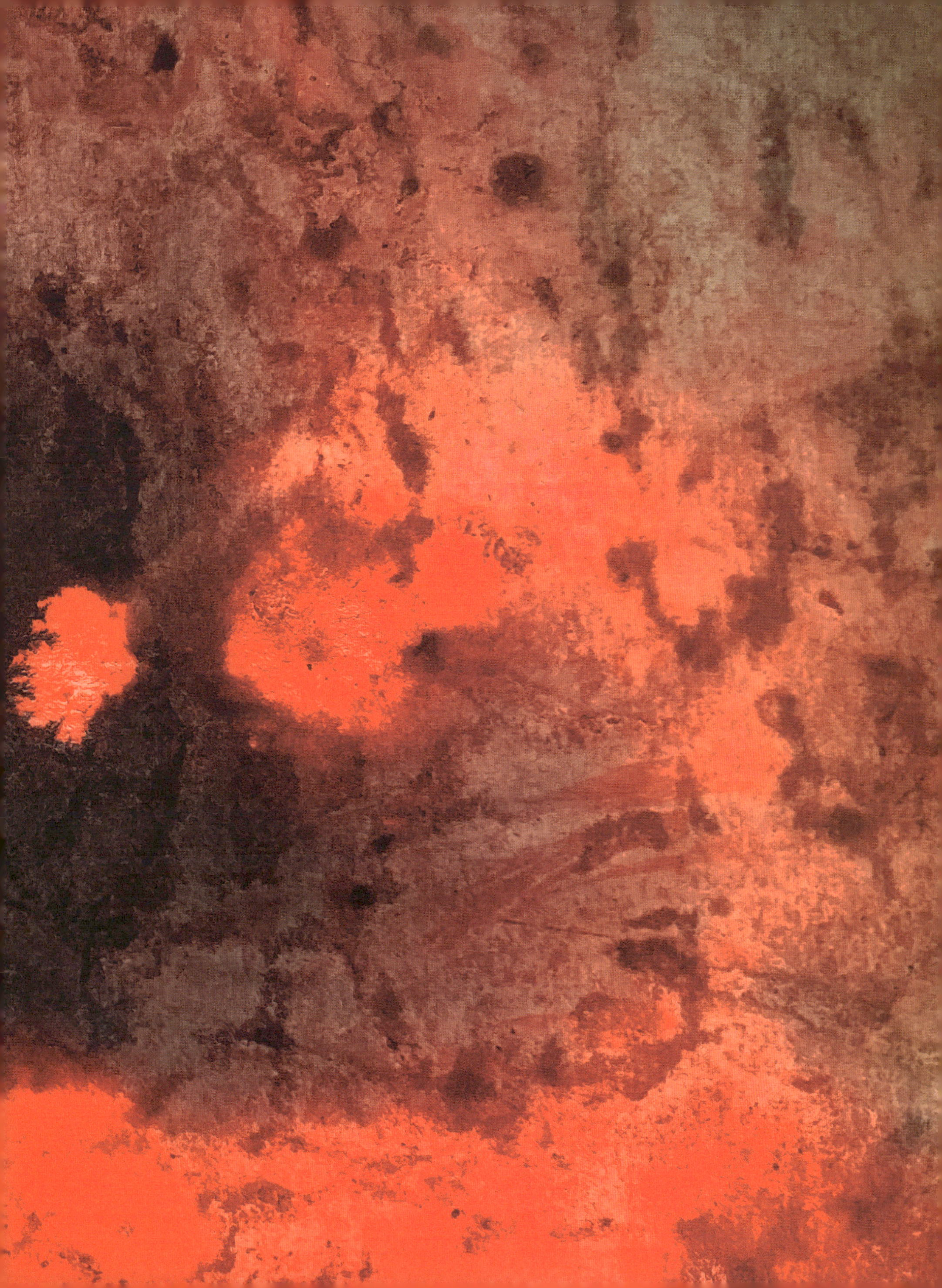

It's said that once the wharenui and pātaka at Ōraka were full such that the doors could no longer close, we convened the full whare wānaka to decide our next steps.

So much of Te Waipounamu was irreplaceable. To many of us, saving some taoka and leaving the rest to chance was unacceptable.

Over six days we agreed to widen the scope of collection until it was clear no building could serve as our ark.

Mahere was the chief advocate of collecting everything, living and dead. It's said that on the seventh day, she stood.

All fell silent.

She crossed the pae to stand at the base of the great wall of the wharenui where the original, digital Ark of Arks was preserved.

She made a fist and thumped it against the side of the pou.

The cavity opened; the Ark of Arks emerged.

She opened the ingenious locks and dumped the contents onto the ground. She had our attention now.

'What is the name of this island?' she called.

'Te Waka o Aoraki,' we replied.

She gestured to the ocean, the hills north and south, the low mountains to the west, the plants and animals, cities and towns, roads and waste dumps, libraries and jails.

'Āe, our tipuna's ark. Already full and already under sail.'

There was little discussion after that. We resolved to count the island and its total contents as our ark.

We declared the wharenui and pātaka unnecessary — blasphemous, even — and set about demolishing them.

Then, one by one, we returned to our homes to await what was coming.

It's said that at this point the faction who wished to collect essences disowned the project and cut all ties.

It's said that even before the destruction of the wharenui and pātaka was complete, this faction built replicas of those imposing and beautiful spaces on the hilltop to the west overlooking the bay.

It's said they decreed that only things reduced to their essence would be permitted inside.

It is said that their whare and pātaka remained empty and in darkness.

◎

TIME IS RUNNING OUT OF --------

◎

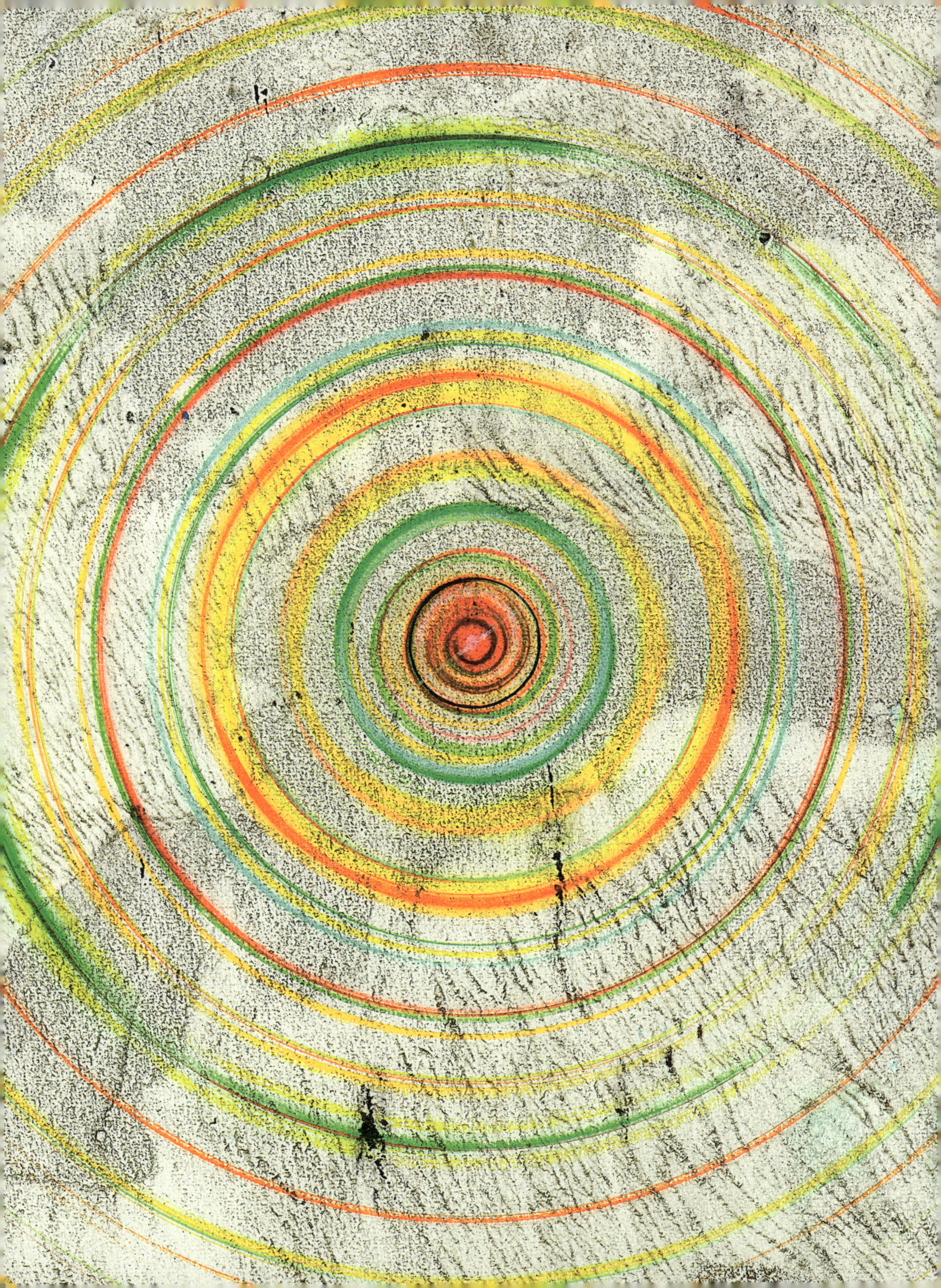

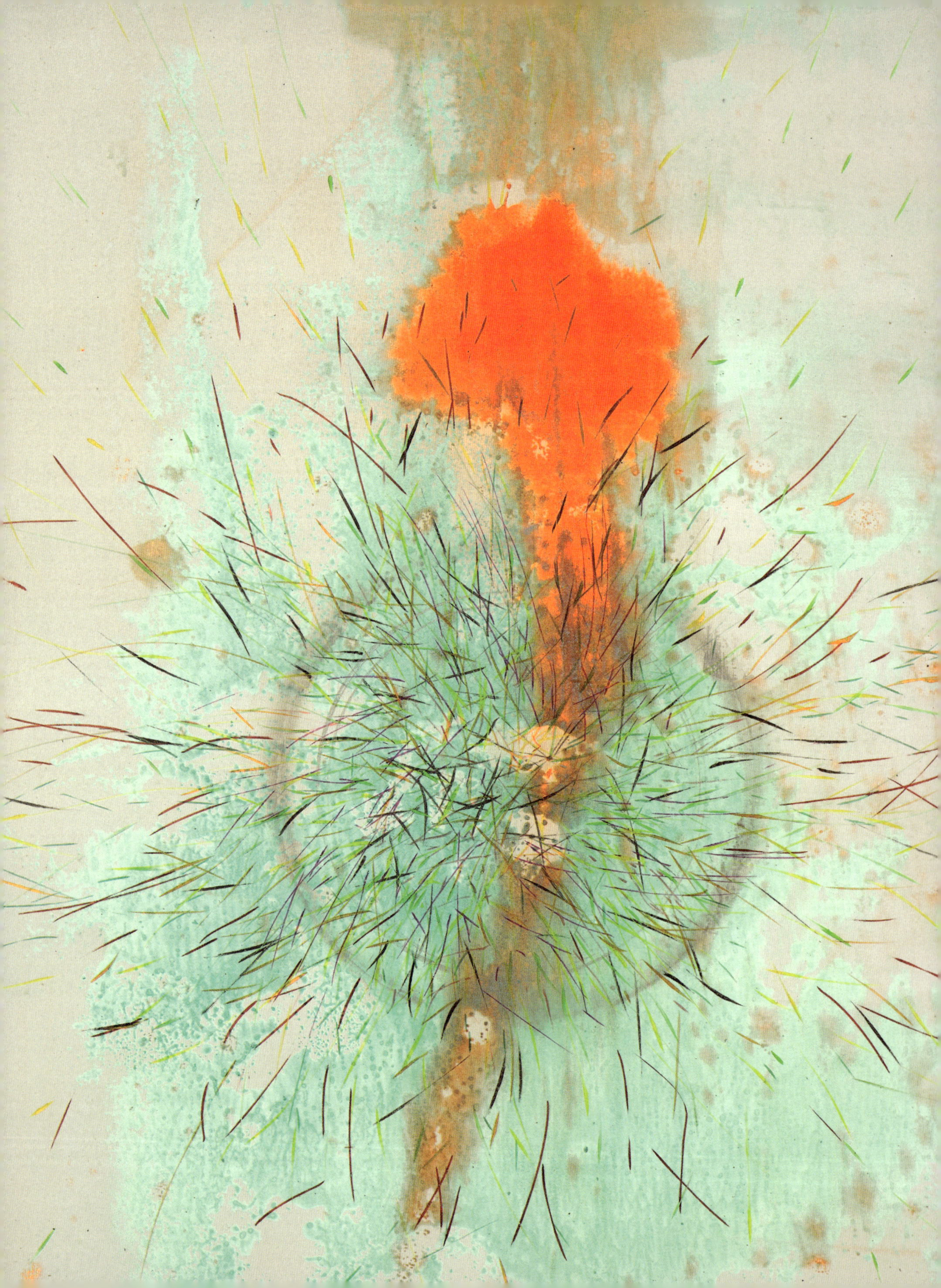

I have visited that darkness: te pō takotako, te pō kerekere. A thick darkness, an intense darkness. A darkness one shade lighter than the void, but only just.

Move past the doorway and the walls disappear. The roof soars overhead, cavernous, then is lost to blackness.

I sat for hours, wondering. I sat for days. For years.

I saw soft pillars of light flicker in and out of being.

I heard one word murmured in a hundred tongues. I understood none, or perhaps all.

I heard the subterranean flickering roar of a pūrerehua, a spinning blade, a wheel the size of the world.

I heard the *om* of a billion billion spinning fans.

When I came to leave, there was no way to leave. I saw the dead living and the unborn dead.

I waited in te pō. I felt the darkness grow warm. Though I could not see them, others waited with me in the night.

One day we would germinate.

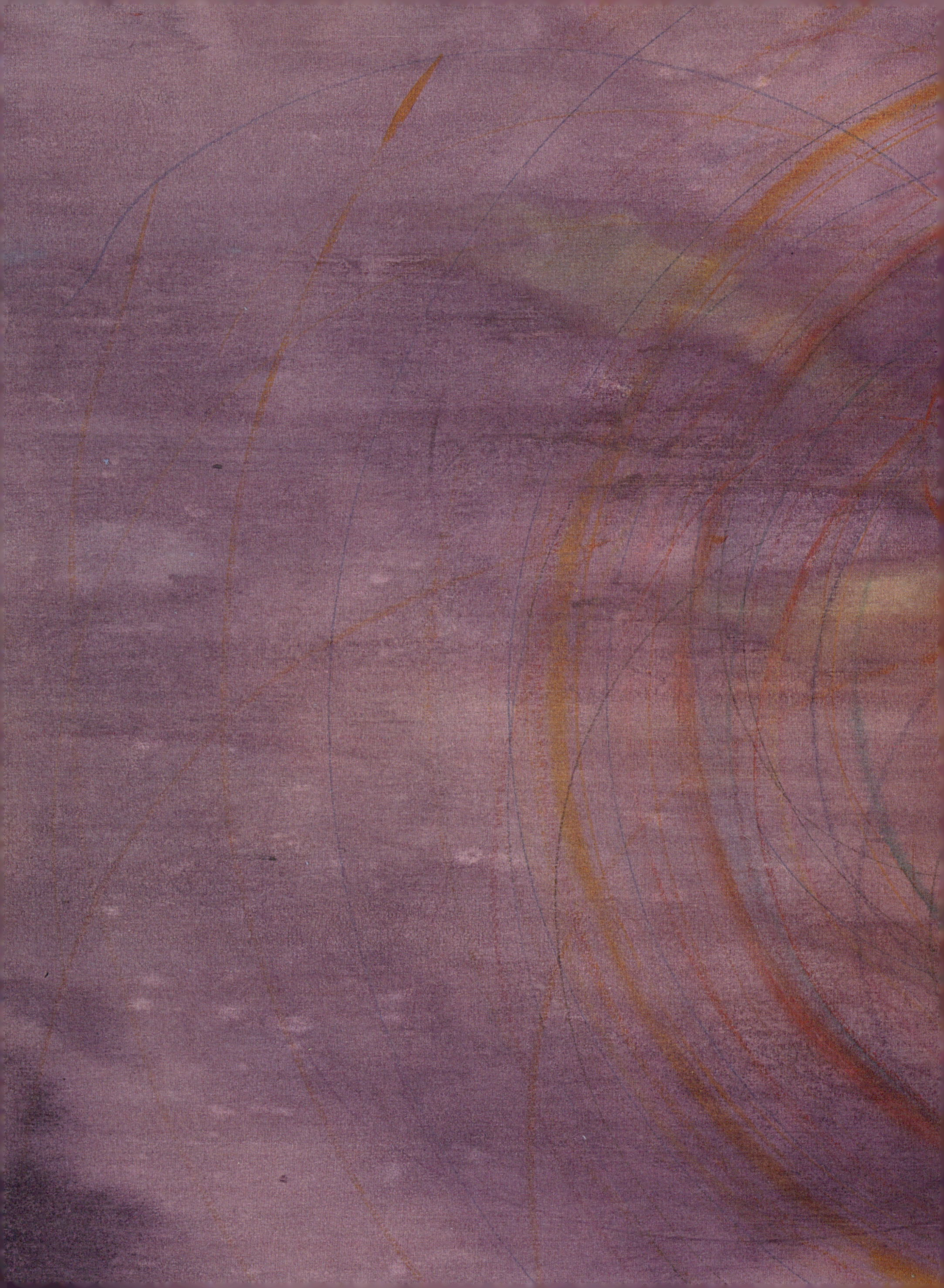

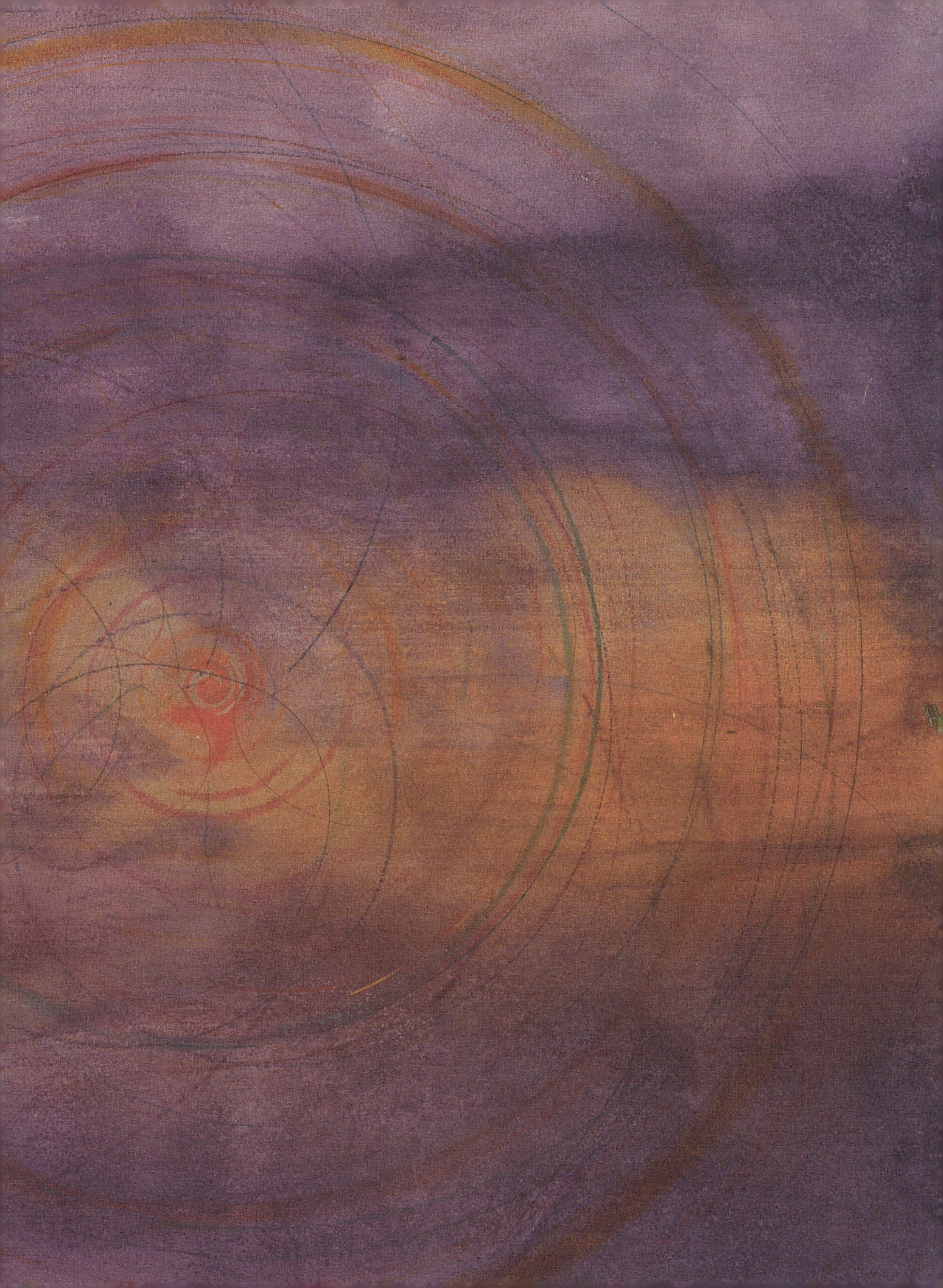

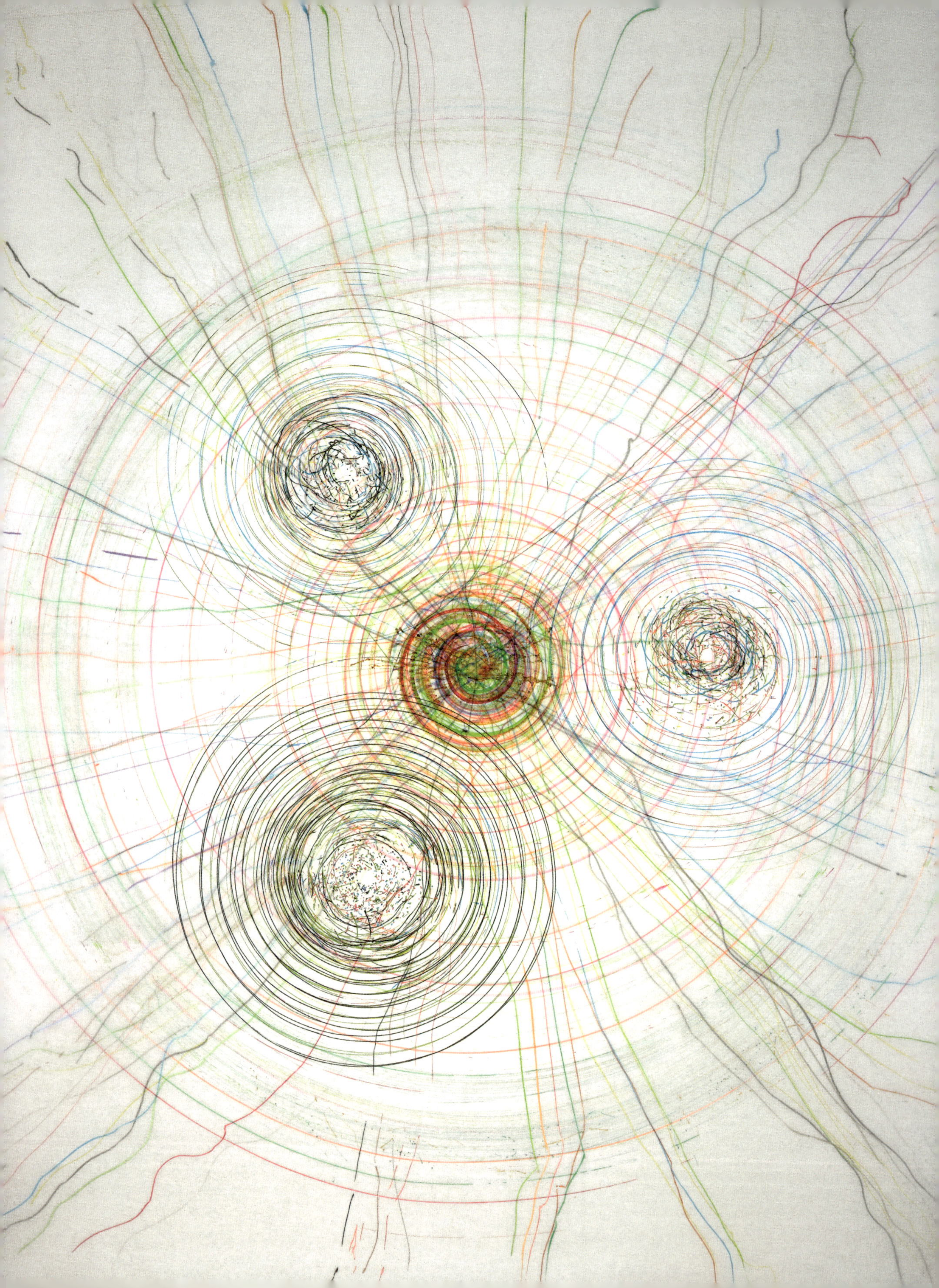

About the contributors

Phil Dadson ONZM is a transdisciplinary artist, musician/composer and improviser, whose practice spans some 50 years. He is the founder of the acclaimed music/performance group From Scratch. He was a lecturer in Intermedia at the Elam School of Fine Arts from 1977 to 2001, when he left to take up full-time art practice. He is a New Zealand Arts Foundation Laureate, and has been awarded an Antarctic Artist Fellowship and a grant from the Fulbright-Wallace Arts Trust. Dadson lives in Tāmaki Makaurau Auckland and is represented by Trish Clark Gallery.

Nic Low (Ngāi Tahu) is the partnerships editor at *NZ Geographic* magazine and the former programme director of WORD Christchurch. An author of short fiction, essays and criticism, his writing on wilderness, technology and race has been widely published and anthologised on both sides of the Tasman. His story collection *Arms Race* (2014) was shortlisted for the Readings Prize and the Queensland Literary Awards. *Uprising* (2021) details his walking expeditions exploring the Ngāi Tahu history of the Southern Alps. It received the CLNZ Writers' Award and the Wily Prize, was shortlisted for the New Zealand Heritage Book Awards, and was named a *New Zealand Listener* and *Australian Book Review* Book of the Year.

Gary Stewart is an Otago-based designer (The Gas Project), who works in identity, packaging and restaurant design, as well as book publication. He is the designer of all the books in the kōrero series.

Little Doomsdays is the fifth book in the kōrero series. The kōrero project invites new and exciting collaborations for two different kinds of artistic intelligence to work away at a shared topic. Other books in the series are *High Wire* (2020), by Lloyd Jones and Euan Macleod; *Shining Land* (2020), by Paula Morris and Haru Sameshima; *The Lobster's Tale* (2021), by Chris Price and Bruce Foster; and *Bordering on Miraculous* (2022), by Lynley Edmeades and Saskia Leek.

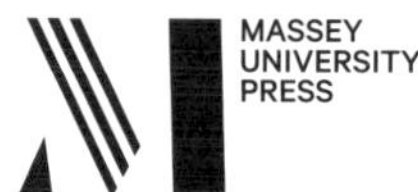

First published in 2023 by Massey University Press
Private Bag 102904, North Shore Mail Centre
Auckland 0745, New Zealand
www.masseypress.ac.nz

Design by Gary Stewart, The Gas Project
Cover illustrations by Phil Dadson

Text page 83: Enheduanna's 'Temple Hymn 7', translation by Betty De Shong Meador with John Carnahan, in *Jacket 2*, 27 June 2017

A catalogue record for this book is available from the National Library of New Zealand

The assistance of Creative New Zealand is gratefully acknowledged by the publisher

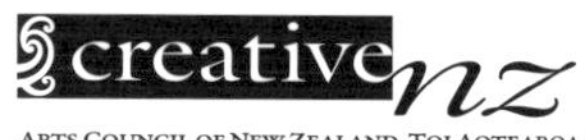

Printed and bound in China by Everbest Investment Ltd

ISBN: 978-1-99-101625-6